Protect Me:
Brie's Submission

By
Red Phoenix

Protect Me: Brie's Submission

Copyright © 2016 by Red Phoenix
Print Edition

RedPhoenix69@live.com

Edited by Amy Parker, Proofed by Becki Wyer & Marilyn Cooper
Cover by CopperLynn
Phoenix symbol by Nicole Delfs

*Previously published as part of *Brie Embraces the Heart of Submission*
Adult Reading Material (18+)

Dedication

MrRed not only supports my writing,
but all my fans as well.
He knows the difference you have made in my life.

To my beautiful fans who have supported and
encouraged me
throughout this incredible journey.
You are truly amazing people in your own right
and it is my joy to know you!

CONTENTS

Unforeseen

B rie entered the gym wearing her special jewelry underneath her sweats. She'd modeled it in the bathroom earlier that morning. It was beautiful, making her look as if she had a clit of gold. None of the blue glass showed—just the shiny jewelry and the thin, black thong with a stylish gold clasp in back. She had twirled several times to admire it from every angle before slipping on her sweatpants.

With each step, her outer lips rubbed against the glass, causing a subtle pressure on her clit and making Brie acutely aware of the jewelry's presence. *I feel you, Sir...* she thought with a smile on her lips as she made her way to the car.

The gym was busy, as was usual that early in the morning. Brie found an unoccupied elliptical and started running.

Oh, the rubbing...

Brie closed her eyes and fantasized about her Sir.

She was bound with her arms high above her.

"Open," he commanded, placing a cloth gag in her

mouth and tying it tightly behind her head. "There will be no kissing or speaking, although you are allowed to moan."

He disappeared from her line of sight. She could hear him rifling through his assortment of instruments and tools, but Sir returned with nothing in his hands.

When he saw her look of surprise, he gave her a sexy smirk. "Don't you remember, Brie? I told you I believe in the power of touch…"

His hands caressed her skin, sending electric flutterings throughout her body. "You've missed your Master's touch, haven't you?"

She nodded, then moaned into her gag when he cupped her breasts and lightly pinched her nipples. He bent down and took one into his mouth. The contact created a deep ache—a desperation to connect, to be filled with him, body and soul.

Brie groaned, pressing herself into him as he began to suck. Sir broke the suction and stood back, smiling mischievously. "I can sense your need. Shall I tease you some more?"

She shook her head, knowing he would not listen to her.

Sir came back to her and slipped his hand between her legs, rolling his finger over her swollen clit. Brie threw her head back and moaned loudly. It wouldn't take much…and then her Master knelt down.

Brie squirmed in her bindings when she felt Sir kiss her clit reverently.

Oh, God, sweet torture!

"So good…" he murmured gruffly. Sir rapidly flicked

his tongue over her clit, setting it on fire with his expertise.

She looked down at his face, buried in her hairless pussy, and felt the stirrings of an orgasm.

Brie started running faster, teasing her clit with the jewelry as she exercised and fantasized for all she was worth.

Make me come, Sir! she cried in her head.

Heart racing, pussy throbbing, she let her fantasy take it up a notch. Sir moved behind her and fingered her anus. "I'm going to fuck your ass, my dear. No foreplay, just good old-fashioned thrusting from a hard cock. Do you think you can handle it?"

Brie nodded, whimpering when he placed his rigid member against her tight hole.

Sir grabbed her waist and, with one solid thrust, forced the length of his cock deep inside her.

Brie let out a small cry when she came.

"Are you all right?"

Brie looked over at the elliptical beside her. It was the stately older woman she had become good acquaintances with. On the second day, Elizabeth had struck up a conversation after they were done exercising. The lady seemed nice and not overly intrusive, so that Brie had come to look forward to their short conversations every morning. It made it that much more embarrassing to be caught orgasming in front of her now.

"I think I might have tweaked a muscle. It's nothing, really," Brie said, trying to control her blush.

"You need to be sure to listen to your body, young lady. Don't overdo it."

"Yes, ma'am." Brie agreed. She increased the resistance on the machine and closed her eyes to shut out the rest of the world. *Sir, I'm so naughty! Do you want me to be naughty again?*

Brie had a satisfied grin on her face by the time she finished up her hour at the gym. She hadn't thought it was possible to maintain a physical relationship while being far apart, but Sir had managed it with this simple trick.

Her imagination had no problem convincing her body the hardness between her legs was Sir's princely cock. Knowing he was fantasizing about her at the same time had been enough to send her over the edge. How incredibly wrong to orgasm in a crowded gym while she was exercising, but she adored the wickedness of it!

Brie got off the machine a sweaty but happy mess. She headed towards the lockers, but stopped cold when she saw Faelan just outside the gym, waiting for her. She looked around, unsure how to avoid a confrontation with the Dom.

"What's wrong? You look like you've seen a ghost," Elizabeth said, joining her at the lockers.

Brie pointed Faelan out to the older woman. "See that man? His name is Todd Wallace and he's stalking me. I can't leave this place until he's gone."

Elizabeth looked him over through the glass door and tsked. "Tell you what. I'll go out there and talk to him. When his back is turned, you scoot over to the coffee shop next door. I'll meet you there when the coast is clear."

It seemed like a reasonable solution. "Okay. But

please, whatever you do, don't let him see me."

Elizabeth put her hand on Brie's shoulder to reassure her. "It'll be a piece of cake. By the way, I'd like a double latte."

Brie nodded dully, trying to keep her fear in check. She had a feeling Faelan would smell it on her.

She watched the elegant woman exit the building and engage Faelan. Brie didn't know what Elizabeth said, but he willingly followed her into the parking lot, away from the entrance. Brie held her breath, walked out of the door and straight into the café.

She didn't allow herself to breathe until she was seated at a table in the back. Both lattes were sitting on the table, getting cold, by the time Elizabeth finally joined her.

The woman sat down gracefully, placing her purse on the empty chair next to her. "You have nothing to worry about, Brianna. That boy was simply waiting for a friend. His name is Tommy. Such a nice lad."

Brie wasn't convinced. "How do you know his name is Tommy? Fae…Todd could have been lying to you."

Elizabeth laughed as she picked up her cup and took a tiny sip. She made a face before setting it back down. "I asked for his driver's license, dear. You're not dealing with an amateur."

Brie was stunned. "How could you possibly get him to show you that?"

The older woman smiled craftily. "I have my ways…"

Brie held up her cup to make a toast. "Thank goodness for friends in unexpected places." She swallowed the lukewarm brew, not minding the temperature.

Elizabeth smiled and clinked mugs with her, but put hers back down without drinking any. "It was my pleasure, Brianna."

In the short time they spent in the café, Brie learned that Elizabeth was the proud owner of a new spa in LA. "I recently moved from New York, where I previously ran a spa called Serenity. All the Broadway stars frequented it; it was truly divine…" she said wistfully. "However, the cold winters finally got to me and I thought LA sounded like a nice place to retire. But I miss my clients, so I started up a sister spa."

It turned out that Elizabeth was single, but seemed quite content as a free agent. "I find I am still too young to settle down. Too many delectable men to enjoy, including that handsome boytoy I just met."

Brie's jaw fell open. "You made a pass at Tommy?"

Her laughter was pleasant, but controlled. "Hell no, honey. *He* made the pass at me."

Brie had to admit the woman oozed confidence and sex appeal, despite the gray in her jet-black hair.

"So what do you do for a living, Brianna?"

Brie sighed in frustration. At this point, her documentary was still under wraps, so she replied, "I'm an unemployed film director. Still trying to make connections so I can get my work noticed."

Elizabeth smiled with perfect crimson lips. "Maybe I can help with that. I see all kinds of high-end clients at my spa. I could put in a good word for you. Do you have any business cards I can pass out?"

Brie was only half listening, wondering, *Really, who*

wears makeup to work out? She dug in her purse, looking for a card. Although she had business cards, they were outdated because of her old address. She handed one over, apologizing as she did so. "The cellphone number and email are correct, but unfortunately the address is not."

Elizabeth's long red nails caught Brie's attention as she took the card. Everything about the woman was meticulously perfect.

Is she a Domme...?

The older woman looked the card over critically. "I have a friend who owns a printing shop. I am sure he could print up a few hundred of these free of charge. Do you have your new address?"

"Actually, I was planning to leave my address off the next set of business cards. It's unnecessary in this day and age. If someone needs to mail me something, they can just message me."

Elizabeth pursed her lips and nodded. "True enough. So would you like me to have new ones printed up? A business card should reflect the professionalism of the person it represents. This screams 'amateur' to me. Ricky would do a far better job."

Even though her critique was unsolicited, Brie had to agree with Elizabeth's assessment. "If it's no trouble, I guess that would work. But I have to ask, why would he do it for free?"

The older woman raised her eyebrow. "Why, in-deed?"

Brie noticed that her new friend had glanced at her collar several times throughout their conversation. She was fairly certain the woman was a Dominatrix. However, Elizabeth made no mention of it. The lady kept the conversation light and short. "Until tomorrow, Brianna. Hopefully you'd be open to doing this again sometime soon, stalker or no stalker."

Brie giggled. "This was nice. Consider it a future date."

"Good," Elizabeth said, as she got up to leave. The lady had a sexy sway to her hips, one that grabbed the attention of a male customer. He got up and opened the door for her, staring at her ass for several seconds before going back to his coffee.

Elizabeth knew how to win over the male population, even in workout clothes.

Brie was surprised that she felt anxious with Tono in the room. She'd been on stage countless times during her training, and she'd been part of several club scenes, but this felt different. These were complete newbies and she could sense their collective nervousness.

She surveyed the class of twenty-four. Most were couples ranging from their twenties into their thirties, but there were several who looked to be in their forties and beyond. It was an interesting range of ages.

Tono had requested Brie only wear a thong underneath her clothing. Once the class was quiet, he introduced the two of them and asked Brie to remove her clothes.

Brie gracefully removed her skirt and blouse, to the quiet gasps of two women in the front row. It reminded her of an art class with a nude model.

She accepted their surprised stares willingly, focusing her attention on Tono to distract herself. He held up his tools for the evening: several bundles of jute and a pair of medical scissors. He then handed out a pair of scissors to each of the students. "This is my gift to you. Keep it within reach whenever you practice the art of Kinbaku."

He went on to share the history of Kinbaku as he unwound a section of jute. He explained how it had morphed from being a form of torture to an erotic exchange between two people.

"Americans often use the term Shibari. It is my personal belief that the two are similar, but different. Shibari focuses on the art—the beautiful image created by the bondage itself. Kinbaku, on the other hand, is about the process—the connection between the couple. It makes no difference to me if you call it Shibari or Kinbaku. However, in my class I will only use the term Kinbaku, with the understanding that your success has less to do with how the bondage looks, and more about how you interact with your partner during the exchange."

Tono turned the flute music on and adjusted it to a soothing background noise. "It is important to create a peaceful setting. One in which your partner can lose herself in the act of binding." He ran his hands over Brie's naked skin as he continued talking. "Contact is essential during the scene. You seduce as you restrain."

He stood behind her and wrapped one arm around her chest, just under her breasts, pressing her against him. "Breathing in sync is an effective tool for connecting." He leaned down and whispered loud enough for them to hear, "Breathe with me, toriko."

Brie smiled as she laid her head back against his shoulder and closed her eyes. Even though it was second nature to sync with him, it immediately calmed her. After a minute or two, Tono pulled away and began to wrap the rope underneath her breasts, where his arm had been moments before. He explained each step as he went, unwinding and redoing as he made the simple chest harness.

His hands lightly brushed her nipples as he worked, keeping them hard and receptive. When he was done, he tightened the harness just a little more, causing her pussy to tingle with need. It didn't matter that he was using basic techniques; Tono knew exactly how to seduce her—and the audience.

He tied her wrists next. "This is visually and emotionally powerful. After you bind your partner in this way, lift her arms above her head. You now have freedom to explore her body with your fingers and the extra length of rope." Tono used the dangling jute from her wrist bindings to lightly slap her skin.

She was intrigued that he was demonstrating techniques he had never used on her before. Brie assumed that it was for the benefit of those who might never proceed further than these simple skills. She loved Tono all the more for it. Although he was a highly experienced Master, he had taken into account the level and comfort of his students.

Tono tied a new section of jute to her chest harness

and brought it between her legs. "Be aware of the amount of pressure you place on her clit. You can take what is meant to be pleasurable and make it unbearably painful if you are not careful. It is necessary to ask your submissive how it feels as you experiment with the tautness of the rope. You can always loosen or tighten based on her response. It is not a sign of weakness; it is an indication of your commitment to her well-being."

Brie moaned softly as he applied just the right amount of pressure with the jute. He turned her around to show the class how to attach the rope in the back, and then positioned her to face the crowd again.

Tono lightly touched her pussy with two of his fingertips as he adjusted the rope. It seemed unintentional, until he explained to the class, "A simple touch in erogenous zones while you work has the power to drive your partner wild."

Brie bit her lip and nodded. She heard giggles coming from some of the ladies in the group. Oh, yes—she knew they wanted him to touch *their* erogenous zones.

Tono handed out a length of jute to each individual in the class. "It is important to know how the jute feels on your own skin, whether you plan to do the binding or have the binding done to you. My first assignment requires you to take off your shoes and socks so that you can bind your own ankles together." There were many nervous chuckles as people followed his instructions.

To demonstrate the procedure, he had Brie sit on a chair. She watched in amusement as the class made humorous attempts to bind themselves according to Tono's directions. Brie noticed there was one female who seemed especially quick to catch on, but the majority had about as much talent as Brie herself did. It was entertaining to watch.

She observed Tono correct and encourage each person individually. His patience was extraordinary. It was truly an honor for Brie to be a part of this introduction to Kinbaku. She wondered if the students understood they had a gifted Master in their midst.

Tono ended the class by untying Brie from the jute with lingering caresses and plenty of kissing. She could feel the sexual tension rise in the room, and suspected many of the couples would be experiencing passionate encounters of their own after class.

He commanded Brie to dress, and then had the class thank her for the demonstration. She blushed at their applause and bowed to Tono.

The applause increased, with a few enthusiastic hollers to round out his accolades. It took a full half-hour before the classroom emptied. His students felt the need to personally thank him before they left. It was gratifying to hear their enthusiasm and impressions of the first night of class.

Brie was surprised when several of the women came over to thank her, as well.

"It was lovely to watch your connection together."

"Miss Toriko, I hope my husband and I can create that kind of harmony."

Brie smiled. "I am sure you will," she encouraged. "The breathing is crucial and very sexy."

"Yes, it was sexy to watch! How long have you two been together?"

Brie wasn't sure how to answer, and chose to willfully misdirect instead. "Actually, this is our first class…"

Once the classroom had cleared out, Tono held out his hand to her. She walked into his embrace and the two simply drank in the joy of the experience.

"This is a good thing, Tono."

"Yes, it is, toriko."

"Thank you for letting me be a part of it."

"The pleasure is mine, little slave."

He picked up the rope and smiled as he bundled each strand. "I am surprised to find that teaching the correct method to those new to the art is as satisfying as teaching advanced skills to the experienced."

"They are lucky to have this opportunity," Brie said, looking forward to next week's class. "Truth is, I feel lucky too."

He kissed her on the lips before handing her the last bundle of jute. "We make a good team, you and I."

She fell into a comfortable routine with Tono that second week. Brie did not live each day in quiet desperation for Sir's return, choosing instead to embrace the unique life experience Tono offered.

However, Brie was still overjoyed when Sunday rolled around, knowing she would get to hear Sir's voice. The day held special excitement because not only was she going to get to speak with Sir in the morning, but she had an interview set up with the girls that afternoon. She had decided they should gather at Mary's apartment, believing the tight-lipped woman would be more open if she was in her own environment. It would also serve to feed Brie's curiosity about what kind of place Mary had.

Just before she left for the gym that morning, Brie inserted the pussy jewelry and rubbed the gold appreciatively. The beautiful piece fit as if it had been made for her, and had the added benefit of teasing her clit with its slight pressure. She decided to wear a half shirt and flattering shorts to match her sexy attire.

Brie left the house quietly, being careful not to wake Tono. She remained silent until she slipped into her car, where she spotted a small pot of purple and yellow flowers sitting on the passenger seat. Brie picked the small pot up and cradled it in her arms. They were crocuses, the flower Sir had mentioned in his poem. She knew their name, having googled it after reading his romantic words.

Brie looked at Tono's home and smiled. She had no idea when he had placed Sir's gift in her car, but she would be sure to thank him on her return.

It thrilled her to have received so many thoughtful gifts from her Master. Not only the sexy jewelry and the romantic poem, but now she could add flowers to the list. She lifted the colorful flowers to her nose and kissed the delicate petals. "I love you, Sir!"

It was with a joyous heart that she pulled up to the workout center with a single crocus tucked behind her ear. But once she entered the building, she stopped dead in her tracks. "It can't be…"

He tilted his head slightly and asked, "It can't be

what?"

Brie didn't waste a second, jumping into his arms with utter abandon. "Sir!"

He held her tight, rocking her back and forth in his embrace. "So you're glad to see me?"

"Best present ever!" she exclaimed. "I got your flowers this morning, but I never dreamed I would see you today."

Still holding her with one hand, he lifted her chin and kissed her in front of everyone in the gym. Her whole body tingled with electricity and for a moment, time stood still as she reveled in their soul connection.

Brie wanted to protest when Sir finally put her back on the ground. He looked down at her tenderly, touching the flower in her hair. She tiptoed to kiss Sir again, but stopped when she noticed the color completely drain from his face.

Sir growled under his breath. "What is *she* doing here?"

The Beast

I n a fluid motion, Sir moved Brie behind him as he stepped forward to face the threat alone. "You have no business being here."

Elizabeth smiled easily, as if she had expected such a negative response. "It's a free country, Thane."

"Who is she?" Brie asked, stunned at Sir's odd behavior towards the woman, suddenly afraid she knew exactly who it was but not able to believe it.

"No one," he answered angrily, taking Brie's hand and turning to leave.

"Are you really such a coward, Thane? I had expected you to grow into a man by now."

The entire gym was now focused on the scene being played out before them.

"Come, Brie," Sir said with forced calm, guiding her towards the door.

Brie was shocked to feel him literally shaking with rage, the air around him rife with hostility. She kept up with his long strides. They were both desperate to get away from the situation as swiftly as possible.

From behind her, she heard, "Don't walk away from your mother, boy."

Sir didn't break his stride as he pushed through the door and shouted, "I have no mother!"

Brie stole a glance back at Elizabeth. The woman lifted her chin and smiled at Brie condescendingly. A cold chill coursed through Brie's veins as she realized how easily she had played into Elizabeth's hands. But she could not fathom how the woman could be Thane's mother. She looked far too young.

"Keys," Sir snapped.

Brie dug the keys out of her pocket and handed them to him. "Sir, I didn't kn—"

"Not now, Brie."

He slid into the driver's seat and she automatically slipped into the passenger side, grabbing onto her flowerpot and clutching it to her chest.

"Seat belt," he barked.

Brie belted herself in as Sir revved the engine loudly and took off with a squeal of tires and black smoke.

He drove like a man possessed, going above the speed limit for the foggy conditions, which were normal that early in the morning. At all times he remained in control, but he drove with a dangerous focus that unnerved her.

Sir did not proceed to their apartment. Instead, he headed for the California hills that overlooked the city. The atmosphere inside the vehicle was alarming. She had never seen Sir so upset. He stared at the road, his jaw set, his eyes narrow—a seething mass of tension. Brie was afraid that if she dared to touch him, he would explode.

She buried her face in the flowers and said a silent prayer.

Sir suddenly pulled off to the side of the road and jumped out of the car. She scrambled out too, unwilling to leave him alone.

He stormed to the edge of a steep embankment and held his arms out wide in the swirling fog, screaming with his fists clenched towards the sky. The sound of his cry broke Brie's heart. It was full of pain on a level she had never experienced. His screams of agony were swallowed up by the surrounding mist.

Sir roared again, but it was full of a rage that frightened her. He looked around wildly and then focused on the hard trunk of a large tree. He began punching the rough surface in blind anger, not caring about the damage he was doing to his fists.

Brie cried out, wanting to stop him but understanding, on a deeper level, his need to unleash the furious wrath within him. After countless sickening thuds, he fell to his knees and slumped against the base of the tree.

She ran to him then, wrapping her arms around Sir, trying to impart every ounce of her strength to him.

Sir wept—a deep, raw release of emotion that had been buried for years. She didn't say anything as she held onto him, needing him to know he was not alone in his grief. Finally the sobs ceased and he became silent. Time stood still in the white mist, silent and cold, while he struggled with his grief and pain.

"I love you," she whispered.

Sir responded by pulling her to him and tucking her into his arms. She lay on the ground, her head buried in his chest. He held her in silence, words unnecessary as he took comfort in her presence. But it wasn't enough to fill the emotional abyss. Sir pulled at her clothes, removing them hurriedly until his fingers met the resistance of her jewelry. He grunted and looked down for a second, ripping it from her and replacing it with his cock.

Sir climbed onto Brie, like a drowning man climbing into a boat. She became his means of survival as he filled the cavernous void in his soul with her feminine offering. Brie opened herself to him, willingly accepting her role. Sir's groans were subdued as he took her deep and hard. Brie looked up at the swirling mist, tears streaming down her face as she cried for Thane the young adolescent and Thane the man.

All that pain, held inside for years, was now exacting an excruciating toll as it erupted with violent force. The desperate coupling seemed to go on forever, his anguish too great for him to find release. Eventually he stiffened inside her and cried out in painful relief.

Sir pushed off her and lay beside Brie on the ground, watching the swirling mist as his breath slowly returned to normal.

When he finally turned to Brie, his anguished gaze penetrated the depths of her soul, causing her to shiver from the chill of it, but she did not flinch.

"Seeing that woman," he said hoarsely, "it's as if it happened yesterday. I see him on the floor, struggling for breath, blood everywhere." Brie felt him shudder beside her. "She just stood there and did nothing, cold as ice." Sir growled as he looked back up at the sky. "It should have been her on the ground. To this day, I wish it had been her."

Brie put her arms around him, but remained silent.

"She wants something from me…"

She pressed against him, wanting to bring comfort and assurance. "Maybe she needs to make amends."

He frowned. "She never showed remorse, never asked for forgiveness. There would be no reason for her to seek it now. I can only think of one thing that would motivate her."

Brie was afraid to voice the obvious question.

Sir continued, speaking his thoughts. "She knew I wouldn't have given her permission to see me…so she went through you." He snorted in anger. "As devious and selfish as I remember."

The mist had slowly given way to the warmth of the sunshine. Sir stared up at the sky as the sun broke through the haze. "It's time we head over to Ren's."

He gently dressed her, as if she were breakable, like china, and then picked up the jewelry and placed it in his pocket. Sir helped Brie to her feet, holding her close for several minutes.

She understood that this had been a significant victory. Sir had survived the unexpected encounter with his mother.

The drive to Tono's was silent but reverent.

Brie wondered if her Asian Master had been told of Sir's early return. Tono's calm expression when he opened the door hinted that Sir had already forewarned him.

"Welcome to my home, Sir Davis," he said.

Brie was technically still Tono's sub and was unsure

how to behave with both Masters. She looked at Sir, who nodded towards him.

Brie bowed. "Tono, how may I serve you?"

"Go change into your normal clothes and pack, tori-ko, while I speak with Sir Davis."

She bowed again before leaving the men. She was excited to be packing to rejoin Sir back at home, but there was a sense of sadness as well. The thought that Tono would face a lonely house after they left hurt her heart.

Brie returned to find them engaged in lively conversation.

"I asked Marquis about Wallace when you told me what happened at the gym. The boy claimed he was nowhere near the workout center the morning Brie saw him."

"Do you believe him?" Tono asked.

"I didn't until this morning."

Brie knelt down at the end of the table between both men.

Sir turned to Brie. "How close were you? Are you certain it was Wallace?"

Brie thought back to that morning and shook her head. "No, Sir. The man looked like Faelan, but I cannot say with one hundred percent certainty it was him."

Sir's face contorted in anger. "Knowing her, I'd be willing to bet it wasn't."

The idea that it hadn't been Faelan blew Brie's mind. "I'm sorry, Sir. I *never* suspected Elizabeth was anything but a kind acquaintance."

"One who now has your business card."

She lowered her eyes. "Yes, Sir."

He lifted her chin. "I do not blame you, Brie. She is a cobra, beautiful to look at but deadly to handle."

Tono sounded appalled. "I was not aware of a business card exchange."

Sir growled angrily. "In a normal world, it would mean nothing. Had I known she was on the prowl again, Ren, I would have insisted you keep Brie with you twenty-four seven."

To Brie he said, "You will have to change your cell phone number and email account immediately. I can assure you, the woman will not leave you alone after this. I may have thwarted her plans, but she will not deviate from her primary goal. She is a tenacious beast."

Brie was disheartened she would not only have to change a phone number she'd had for years, but she would also have to inform everyone of the changes to both accounts. She felt like an idiot.

"What does she want?" Tono asked Sir.

"It's simple—money."

Tono was silent. When he spoke next, his voice was full of compassion. "It is unfortunate that you must deal with such a creature."

Sir's nostrils flared. "Yes, but I will *not* allow her to ruin my life a second time. I would prefer it if you would not mention her to anyone. The fewer people involved, the better."

"It shall remain between us." Tono glanced up at the clock on the wall and informed him, "I do not know if you are aware that toriko has a meeting in four hours, with Ms. Taylor and Miss Wilson."

Brie quickly assured him, "I will reschedule it, Sir."

"No! I do not want my early return to interfere with your plans. You will do the interview as scheduled."

Brie couldn't stand the thought of Sir being alone, today of all days. "Sir, it is no—"

"Brie, you will do the interviews as planned," he stated firmly.

She bowed her head, realizing she had offended him. "Of course, Sir."

Tono addressed Brie. "Toriko, I will need a model for this week's class, since you will not be available to attend. Is there someone you would recommend as your replacement?"

Brie was disappointed she would not be joining Tono's Kinbaku class, but she knew who would make a fine stand-in. "I think Lea would do well."

"Naturally you would suggest Lea," Tono said with amusement. "However, I agree and can see her being a good choice. I'll see if she has any interest."

Dang, that Lea! Brie thought with a grin. *She's so going to owe me...*

Tono stood up and moved to the center of the room, calling Brie to join him.

She looked into his chocolaty brown eyes with a sense of sorrow. As much as she was anxious to be with Sir, her time with Tono had been emotionally profound.

"Give me your wrist, toriko."

Brie held up her wrist to him and watched as Tono untied the jute that signified his ownership. He turned her palm upward and kissed her wrist tenderly. "I release you."

Brie knelt down and bowed her head. "Thank you, Tono. It was an honor to serve you."

He put his hand on her head. "I return you to your Master's service."

Brie felt a physical lifting as he took his hand from her. She stood up and bowed one last time as a sign of her utmost respect for the Dom.

"Brie," Sir called to her.

She returned to him and knelt at Sir's feet. When his hand touched the crown of her head, a jolt of electricity coursed through her. "Stand before your Master."

When she stood up, Brie looked into his eyes. She could see the inner struggle he was attempting to hide. "What is your pleasure, Master?"

"Gather your things. We are leaving."

Tono handed her the small suitcase and her wrist tie. She smiled as she closed her fingers around it. She would keep it as a memento, a reminder of the lessons she had learned under his care.

"Serve your Master well," he said with finality.

The dynamic had officially changed. "I will, Tono Nosaka. I will not forget the lessons you have taught me."

"Good." To Sir, he added, "If assistance is needed in any capacity, do not hesitate to call."

Sir took his hand and shook it warmly. "I will keep that in mind, Ren. Thank you. Your help and support will not be forgotten."

Opening the door to their apartment was the best feeling in the world! Despite having been abandoned for two weeks, his place still held the faint aroma of Sir. Brie took in the smell with relish. *Home…*

"Brie, it was a long flight and I am exhausted," he said gruffly, guiding her towards the bedroom. "Take off your clothes and lie in bed."

She did so dutifully, wondering what he would ask of her. Sir pulled Brie into his embrace once he joined her on the bed. There was no animalistic coupling, no emotional exchange—nothing. He simply fell asleep with her cradled in his arms.

It gave her great joy to be his safe haven. "I will always be that for you, Sir. Always…" she whispered passionately.

Girl Chat

Lea gave Brie a huge hug later that afternoon, when they met outside Mary's apartment.

"Guess who I got a call from!" Lea gushed.

Brie smiled as she started gathering her camera equipment from the car. "A Kinbaku Master?"

Lea eagerly grabbed one of the light reflectors to help her. "Yes! Oh-em-gee, Brie! I cannot believe it. Tono Nosaka called me an hour ago and asked if I would work with him. Can I just say that knowing you is the best thing that has ever happened to me?"

Brie giggled. "I'm glad you're happy, Lea."

"Tell me how I can repay you. I'll do anything—just name it," Lea exclaimed, beaming with happiness.

Since Brie's arms were full, she asked, "How 'bout you ring the doorbell?"

"You got it!" Lea did a graceful pirouette before ringing the bell.

Despite only having a small apartment, Mary took her sweet time to answer the door, asking before she opened it, "Who is it?" as if she wasn't expecting them.

Lea immediately answered, "It's the plumber. I've come to fix the sink."

Mary swung the door open and looked at Lea oddly.

Brie knew the cartoon skit Lea was quoting was a favorite of hers, so she explained to Mary, "You're supposed to say 'who is it?' again."

Mary frowned, but gave in to Lea's puppy dog look. "Fine. Who is it?"

Lea said in a louder voice, "It's the plumber. I've come to fix the sink."

Mary ignored Lea and turned back to Brie, stating in an uninterested voice, "I don't get it."

"You have to ask again."

Mary didn't even crack a smile as she repeated the question one last time.

Lea gasped out the words, "It's the plumber... I've come to fix...the sink." She grabbed her chest, twirled around several times before falling to the ground, 'dead'.

Mary stared at her momentarily, and then said to Brie, "Come in."

Brie giggled as she stepped over Lea's prostrate body and entered Mary's apartment.

Mary shut the door and locked it, leaving Lea lying outside on her doorstep. "Glad I have one less idiot to entertain."

"Hey!" Lea yelled from outside.

Mary walked over to her sofa and sat down with a self-satisfied smile.

Lea began pounding on the door. "Let me in, guys!"

Although Brie thought it was humorous, she took pity on her friend and unlocked the door.

"Party pooper," Mary complained.

"Look, I need both of you for this interview."

Lea pouted. "Didn't you think it was the least bit funny?"

"No!" Mary answered emphatically.

Lea looked at Brie for support.

"Well, it was funny the first time you did it to me. Not so much today."

Lea grabbed her chest, twirled several times and collapsed on the floor.

"Nope, not any funnier," Brie replied.

Lea got up in a huff. "You two have no sense of humor."

"Trust me, Lea. It's you, not us," Mary stated. "There is nothing funny about that."

"That's because you don't know the cartoon," Lea said earnestly. "You see, there's this parrot in the house. The plumber knocks on the door and the parrot asks, 'Who is it?' The plumber keeps answering until he finally gets so frustrated, he has a heart attack. It's an old rerun of Electric Company I used to watch with my dad."

"That explains it," Mary said.

Lea looked at her questioningly. "Explains what?"

"You dad is as much of an idiot as you are."

Lea's face contorted into an ugly scowl as she got ready to let loose on Mary. It was the last thing Brie needed, so she piped up, "Hey, Mary, you got anything to drink?"

Mary shrugged. "Only rum and Coke."

Brie groaned, remembering the last time she had had that particular drink was at the Kinky Goat. It brought a wave of bad memories, but it was the quickest way she could think of to relax the tension in the room. "Make it a double."

Mary turned to Lea. "And you?"

"Make mine a triple. It's the only way I'll be able to stand you."

Brie laughed, thinking back on their first outing together. Despite the passage of time, not much had really changed between the girls.

Mary took care of the drinks, which gave Brie a chance to examine Mary's apartment. She was shocked to see a wide variety of Disney mementos, from little music boxes and posters to pillows and snow globes, all scattered throughout the room. It reminded her of a little girl's bedroom rather than an adult's apartment.

Brie picked up one of the snow globes and watched the glitter swirl around the little redheaded mermaid. When Mary came back with their drinks, Brie asked, "So you're into Disney, huh?"

Mary gave her a nasty look. "Yeah. You got a problem with that?"

"No. It just isn't something I would have expected from such a tough bitch like you."

Mary's expression softened as she handed Brie the drink and took the globe from her. "I love everything Disney. I'm a serious collector."

Lea glanced around the room. "No doubt! I'd say you're like a crazy obsessive collector."

Before Mary could take offense, Brie held up her glass. "Here's to the Three Musketeers—Mary the Mediocre, Lea the Lame and Brie the Beloved."

"Brie the Bitch is more like it," Mary snapped.

Lea rolled her eyes. "Mary, you show no spark of creativity. Clearly, it's Brie the Butt."

All three laughed as they clinked glasses, and Brie forced down Mary's favorite drink. She hid her shudder as she swallowed it, and then got to work setting up the camera and light reflectors while the other two chatted. She focused on the moment instead of on Sir, whom she had left at the apartment all alone. It had nearly killed her to leave him.

"Okay, my plan is to keep things the same as we've always done. We're simply going to sit and talk like we used to after every session. No need to notice the camera. This is just about subbies getting together to dish."

Mary nodded her approval. "Good. I would have punched you in the throat if you'd tried to get a close-up of a tear or something."

Lea laughed. "Are you even capable of crying, Mary?"

"No, that ability died long ago," she quipped, taking a sip of her drink.

It was an honest answer given lightly, but with deep significance. Brie instantly thought of the little girl Mary had once been, and her heart ached for her. This was going to be a difficult interview. She hoped Mary would be resilient enough to survive it.

The girls started off talking about silly things to break the ice, but soon the conversation turned to a serious topic when Mary brought up Brie's time with Tono. "So...how is it living with the Master of the freakish rope tricks?"

Brie smiled. "Tono has been a wonderful Master to me."

"Did he tie you up nice and tight and fuck you silly?" Lea asked.

"He tied me up all right, but I only got a spanking."

Lea giggled. "A spanking? I never thought Tono had it in him."

Mary interjected, "Of course he does. He was doing an excellent job with my spy fantasy just before I had my little 'episode'."

Brie suddenly felt the urge to share. "Mary, you should know that Tono became visibly upset when your breakdown was mentioned while he was watching the documentary."

Mary closed her eyes. "Yeah, whatever."

"Why would it surprise you that he cares about you?"

Mary pursed her lips. "The guy never knew me. Must have been a kneejerk reaction."

Brie was offended by her brush-off of Tono. "He is a genuine person, damn it. Don't you dare belittle his heart."

Mary held up her hands. "Don't get all weird on me Brie. I didn't mean to put down Rope Freak."

"Why do you have to make everything a joke?" Brie complained.

Mary stared at her without speaking, but then sighed deeply and answered, "I…I'm not used to it, don't trust it."

Lea said what Brie was thinking. "Do *not* base your opinion of the male population on your father. He was a fucked-up piece of shit."

Mary held up her glass. "Yes, he was."

"Do you still have contact with him?" Brie asked.

Mary threw her head back and laughed. "Fuck, no! Do you think I'm crazy?"

Brie forged onward with a more difficult question. "What do you think his reaction will be when this film comes out?"

"He won't care. The guy never cared about me, good or bad. I was just his punching bag after my mom left. There isn't a shred of human kindness in that man. He's a worthless excuse of manmeat, take my word for it."

Brie clinked glasses with her. "Okay, he's worthless manmeat. But surely someone had to have been looking out for you as a kid."

The color drained from Mary's face. She looked like she was about to clam up, but then she gulped down her drink and spoke. "In second grade, I told my teacher. She treated me like I was lying to get attention. You know what she said?" Her voice changed as she imitated the woman's voice. "'Your father is under a lot of pressure, young lady.'"

Lea put her hand to her mouth in shock. "No way…"

"I didn't say anything after that, but damn if my third grade teacher noticed the day I cringed after she touched my arm. I told her everything and two weeks later Social Services came to our home. My dad played everything off as if I was a klutzy kid, and they bought it. The fucking social worker bought it hook, line, and sinker."

Brie looked at her with compassion. "I can't imagine

how that must have felt, Mary. Finally being heard and then having it all fall apart."

Mary snarled. "It hurt like fucking hell, bitch! He beat the crap out of me and told me if anyone noticed this time, he would find new ways to hurt me." Mary downed the rest of her drink in one gulp. "I never told another living soul after that, until I was forced to explain what happened with Tono."

Brie asked a harder question, concerned that Mary might not respond but feeling it was important to ask. "How do you feel your childhood experience shaped you as an adult?"

Mary's resistance dissolved as she let out a faint, anguished cry, turning away from them both. "Truth? I'm damaged goods."

The vulnerability Mary exhibited tore at Brie's heart. She put her arm around her and whispered so the camera wouldn't catch it. "You are the strongest woman I know. He did not break you. You not only survived, you overcame his brutality."

Mary shrugged off her hug, but said under her breath, "Thanks." She got up and headed to the kitchen to make another drink before returning. "What else do you want to know? Have at it, bitches. This is your only chance."

Lea piped up, "So did you become a masochist because of your dad?"

"No!" Mary growled angrily. "I hate that you would assume that."

Brie had also presumed that was the case. "Can you explain?"

"I am not a masochist. I don't *like* pain, but I endure it. It's like I have a driving need to defeat it. Like..." She let out a long, ragged breath. "If I was able to bear it without fear, I would finally be the victor over him."

Brie felt tears burn her eyes but Mary glared at her, letting her know that such an emotional response was not acceptable. Brie switched her mindset to that of a director and asked, "So what attracted you to the D/s lifestyle, then?"

Mary held her chin up. "In submission, I find control. It's the only time I have power over my past."

"Wow, that is really profound," Lea said in awe. Mary just rolled her eyes.

Brie was equally impressed, but kept it to herself. Nothing but an indifferent reaction would satisfy Mary. She turned to Lea. "What about you, Lea? What made you want to become a submissive?"

"Well...I am adventurous by nature. I want to try it *all*, nothing held back. In D/s, I find equally adventuresome souls. It's exciting! Anything and everything is allowed as long as we both agree. I don't care how weird it is—I want to try everything at least once!"

"You're a twit, Lea," Mary stated. "Everyone has their limits. You can't convince me otherwise."

Lea grinned at her enthusiastically. "Well, I haven't found mine yet. Sure, there have been a few things I won't try again, but all of it has been interesting. Wouldn't change a thing."

Brie had to ask, "So how will your parents react when you tell them about this film, Lea?"

Her bosom suddenly blossomed a nice, deep shade

of pink that crept all the way to her cheeks. "Well...I'm not sure. My parents have always been my biggest supporters. They're the ones who've encouraged me to explore the world." She looked at the camera guiltily. "I think... I believe they'll be surprised that this is the direction I have chosen, but I don't expect they will love me any less."

Mary stepped in. "What about you, Brie? How will *your* parents handle their perfect little girl going all kinky on them?"

Brie choked on the horrid rum and Coke she was drinking. She hadn't counted on being on the other end of the interview. "My parents? Um... They won't handle it very well. It'll be embarrassing for them, living in a small community with small town values and all. But I trust, as much as it will be a struggle for both my mom and dad, that in the end they will support my decision. Like most parents, their greatest desire is my happiness. Well..." Brie shrugged and grinned. "I've never been happier in all my life."

"Of course," Mary said condescendingly. "'Oh, Brie, our little baby who can do no wrong.'"

Brie snapped at her, "It's not like that at all! I know the news is going to hurt them, but I have to believe they will eventually come around because they love me, and I hold to the belief that love conquers all."

Mary grabbed a pillow in the shape of Pumbaa, the warthog, and hugged it to her chest. "I have a theory. People who are given lots of love as kids attract lots of love. Those who never received it will never know its power."

"What a depressing way to go through life," Lea complained.

But Brie felt only sympathy for Mary. "Haven't you ever loved someone?"

Mary hugged the pillow even harder. "Possibly…" Her vinegar tone returned as she announced, "But it was unceremoniously rejected, which totally proves my point."

Brie wondered if she was speaking about Faelan. The fact Mary would bring it up a second time was significant. Rather than risking embarrassing her on camera by exposing her crush, Brie asked, "So have either of you considered settling down with one Dom now that you've had time to check out what's out there?"

Brie was pretty sure she knew the answer, but felt the viewers would be interested in their responses.

Lea giggled. "Are you kidding, Brie? I love being a submissive for the Center's Dominant training. It is so sweet seeing the new Doms come in, a little unsure of themselves, but leave full of confidence about their calling. It's so damn sexy!"

"But there's no one you would like to settle down with, Lea?" Brie pressed.

She made a pretty little pout. "Maybe, but I'm not sharing who with the rest of the world." She stuck her tongue out at Brie.

Brie laughed and then turned to Mary. "What about you?"

For the first time, Mary did not have a smart comeback. She just shook her head and looked away, sipping at her drink.

Brie took the attention away from her, grateful for Mary's candidness. "I'm still ecstatic with my choice of Dom." She sighed happily and hugged herself.

"So Brie, how does it differ having a twenty-four seven relationship?" Lea asked.

Brie appreciated the chance to share her experience on film. "During training it was more about succeeding in the scene, wanting to get the most out of it. But having this one-on-one interaction with my Master on a daily basis has brought a level of depth to our relationship I never thought possible."

"You're one lucky bitch," Mary grumbled into her glass.

Brie smiled at her with encouragement. "I've said it before, but I believe you and I are a lot alike. Your day will come, Mary, you just have to own it."

"Thank you, Pollyanna," Mary huffed, getting up to mix another drink. "Always sweetness and light, sweetness and light…"

It hurt to have Mary throw her heartfelt words back in her face, so Brie responded with spite. "It is not all sweetness and light, bitch. It is hard to integrate two lives on such an intimate level. Both Sir and I have struggled, but it's because of those struggles that we have grown stronger."

"Can I just say how sick I am of hearing about your perfect life? Fucking sick of it!" Mary spat back.

Lea stepped in to defend Brie, as she had in the past. "Mary, being jealous of Brie is pathetic. In the end, you create the life you have. Despite your father, your crappy childhood, and some idiot who didn't love you back, this is *your* life! You decide today how the rest of your days will play out."

Brie was left speechless. Instead of making a stupid joke, Lea had laid out a sobering truth.

"That's it!" Mary threw the pillow across the room. "I don't have to listen to any more of this shit. Get the fuck out of my apartment, both of you. Now!"

Brie put her drink down slowly, unsure if Mary was serious—but the woman was deadly serious. Mary manhandled Brie off the couch. "I said get out!"

Lea helped Brie gather her camera equipment while Mary went on a cussing spree, the likes of which Brie had never known.

It was with great relief that they made it out, just as Mary slammed the door behind them. "Never again!" Mary screamed from behind the door. "I am never trusting you two bitches again!" Brie heard the lock slide into place.

Lea shook her head at Brie. "What the fuck?"

Brie shrugged her shoulders. "I think we must have touched on some of her greatest fears. I feel terrible, Lea. She opened up so much today, and now she's in there hurting and feeling more alone than ever."

"It's her own fault, damn it," Lea retorted.

"Yes, but she was trying to reach out today. I hate that it ended this way."

"Ain't nobody gonna be able to help that bitch."

Brie frowned. "I refuse to believe that, Lea. Everyone deserves happiness, especially someone as wounded as Mary."

Lea put her arm around Brie. "You can't save the

world, girlfriend. You're just going to get hurt if you try. Rabid dogs bite the hand that tries to comfort them, and Mary is as rabid as they come."

Brie laid her head on Lea's inviting bosom and accepted her hug. "Why don't you tell me a joke?"

"Yay!" Lea squeezed her tighter. "So, you know you've got a serious kink if, while driving up a mountain pass, you read a sign that says 'Chains required' and the first thing that pops into your head is, 'Are whips optional?'"

"I love you and your stupid jokes, Lea," Brie chuckled as she looked at Mary's window. *And I love you too, Mary the Mediocre. Don't you dare give up—bitch!*

Tender Revelation

B rie let the unpleasant ending of the interview fall away from her as she raced back home to Sir. She hadn't told her friends that he was even home, wanting that secret to remain hers a while longer.

She entered their apartment and was startled to see that it was dark. Had he escaped the solitude of the place and gone somewhere else? She was about to call out Sir's name when she heard his voice. "Put your camera equipment down on the floor and strip where you stand."

Brie's heart fluttered as she hurried to do his bidding. She closed her eyes, holding back the tears, realizing how much she'd missed his authoritative sensuality.

"Kneel on the ground, put your shoulders on the floor and spread your arms on either side of you."

A chill went through her as her breasts made contact with the cold marble. She hid her smile in her long hair as she lay there waiting, listening...

She heard the soft clink of glass and imagined him sitting at the kitchen table, enjoying his martini while he made her await his next command. The anticipation rendered her wet and ready.

He prolonged the moment. Brie assumed he enjoyed the temporary postponement of their desires as much as she did.

When she heard him stand and start walking towards her, Brie let out a soft whimper of excitement. His stride was confident and strong, making her loins ache for him.

Sir stood before her, not saying a word.

Brie held her breath, waiting for his next order.

"Don't move," was his only command.

Her body trembled as he stepped behind Brie. "Such a fine ass."

"Thank you, Sir," she whispered.

He lightly ran his fingers over her round curves and said, "I shall partake of it tonight."

She shivered in delight.

"Stand."

Brie stood up and he pressed himself against her. "Put this on."

Brie bit her lip when she saw that it was the pussy jewelry he had given her while he was in Russia. She took it from him, stepped into the thong-like ornament and eased the blue glass into her opening until the outer piece was snug against her clit. He leaned over her shoulder and stroked her golden femininity.

She laid her head back and moaned in response.

He kissed her shoulder. "Hold your hair up, téa."

Brie held up her brown curls and gasped when he undid the collar around her neck. She wanted to protest, but held her tongue. Sir replaced it with a heavy leather collar with a steel ring at the front. The smell of the leather and the weight of the collar were intoxicating.

He attached a leash to the ring, the snap of the metal causing her loins to contract in sexual anticipation. He eased her hands down, biting her earlobe sensually before lightly yanking on the chain, escorting her out of the hallway and into the living room. "Come, téa."

She followed him to the Tantra chair, feeling light-headed. To be with her Master in his apartment again was a dream come true.

Sir knelt down and secured the chain to the leg of the chaise longue, then instructed her to lay her stomach against the lower curve of the chair so that her ass was in the air.

Brie glided over the smooth leather with catlike grace, the chain jingling pleasantly as she did so. She turned her head to watch their reflection in the glass of the expansive window.

She observed Sir slowly undress. Each piece of clothing he stripped off revealed more of his handsome physique, from his toned chest to his firm thighs. She held her breath as he removed his briefs and she glimpsed the extent of his arousal.

Sir glanced up and caught her staring. She immediately lowered her eyes, but he told her, "I want you to watch, téa. Watch your Master dominate this body he has longed to play with for two weeks."

She raised her gaze again and visually worshipped the body of her Master. She adored the hair that covered his chest and the dark patch of pubic hair that framed his manhood. In every way, he was masculine and erotic.

He ran his hands over her smooth skin, lighting her senses on fire. Two weeks apart had made her body desperate for him. Goosebumps covered her skin—her need was so great.

Sir picked up something from the side table and she watched him massage his cock with lubricant. She let out a little gasp, her body anticipating the delicious plundering about to take place.

He caressed her ass with his slippery hands, moving the tiny string that held the jewelry in place out of the way before coating her in preparation for his taking. "Are you ready for me, téa?"

She whispered, "So ready, Master."

Sir wiped his hands on a towel before he laid his body on top of hers, resting his shaft in the valley of her ass. "My cock is going to find its way," he growled in her ear.

Brie watched their reflection as Sir rolled his hips, rubbing his shaft against her sensitive sphincter. He teased her as he hovered over the area and then slipped on by, again and again.

She whimpered softly but did not move, loving the frustration of his roguish teasing. He played with her until her body ached to be filled. She moaned when he changed angles and his rigid cock pressed hard against her taut hole.

Because of the addition of the jewelry filling her pussy, the round head of his manhood seemed much too big for the access he demanded, but they both knew how eagerly she would grant it. The tight outer muscle eventually gave way to his insistent pressure, and Sir pushed himself in. Brie watched his progress in the reflectionin the as he controlled the speed and depth of his cock.

His satisfied sigh made her quiver inside. Nothing was as thrilling as pleasing Master, especially in this intimate way.

"Oh, téa…"

The way she was lying on the Tantra chair gave her no leverage to push against his gentle thrusts. She was completely at his mercy and whim—the collar and chain emphasizing that fact in a primal way. She was suddenly reminded of the brand in the closet and asked hesitantly, "If you were to brand me, Master, where would you put it?"

He grunted, placing his fingers just above her tailbone and caressing the area lightly. Her pussy contracted in fear and longing. The idea of being permanently marked as his was exciting, but the pain…the agony of burning flesh still frightened her.

Sir leaned down and bit her shoulder, deep enough to leave teeth marks without breaking the skin. Brie moaned as her pussy pulsated in an impending orgasm. She shifted slightly, to stave off the pleasure.

"Good girl," he whispered, as he thrust even deeper.

Brie closed her eyes, concentrating every fiber of her being on the friction of his cock rubbing against the tight constriction of her ass, as the jewelry inside moved with each thrust and teased her clit in the process. In this position, with the added pressure of Sir's jewelry, she felt the first flutterings of subspace.

Sir's demanding, yet sensual contact, his confident

domination of her, and the delicate, clinking chain at her neck started a tingling sensation she associated with flight. "I love my Master," she purred.

"Your Master loves you," he replied, giving more emphasis to every thrust.

Brie started moaning softly, hardly aware she was making noises as she let their connection carry her away. She was floating on a cloud of pleasure, content in the love that surrounded her.

He wrapped his hand around her throat, just under her chin, and lifted her head back, kissing her forehead. "This man loves you."

Sir released the warmth of his come inside her, causing Brie to cry out in pure ecstasy, taking her even higher. She let out a long sigh of total bliss, unable to respond to his declaration of love. Her body answered for her, coming around his shaft in loving adulation.

Soon after, he pulled out and repositioned the little string. He unbuckled the leather collar and replaced it with the original silver one. Brie's soul lifted when she heard the gratifying click of the lock, signifying their commitment to each other. Sir picked her up and carried her to the bedroom. Neither spoke, both riding the emotional wave of their connection.

Sir placed her gently on the bed and lay beside her, lightly playing with a strand of her hair. "I have not felt this whole in a long, long time."

She smiled, thrilled that her love had the power to heal.

Although he had been staring at her, his focus moved past her as he spoke. "Seeing her again, although painful, has brought back a flood of memories for me."

"I can only imagine, Sir."

"Would you like to see a picture of him?"

"Please."

He jumped off the bed and rifled through his closet, coming out a minute later with a framed picture. He handed it to her as he lay back down on the bed, putting his arm around her.

It looked like a professional shot taken for a magazine. Alonzo Davis had had long, dark hair and bronze skin. His face had been striking, but it was his eyes that riveted Brie. It was as if she was looking into Sir's eyes. She let out a gasp of surprise.

"Not what you were expecting?" he asked.

"I didn't expect to see so much of you in him."

"Actually, it would be the other way around," he said, chuckling as he took the photo from her and stared at it intently.

"He must have been very popular with his female fans," Brie complimented, touching the picture reverently. "He was an extremely handsome man."

He agreed, "My father had a legion of concert groupies. Women who went to every event—some who even sent him their panties in the mail. But he only had eyes for my mother. His fans respected him for that."

Sir put the photograph on the bedside table, facedown, and lay back on the pillow. "But my mother managed to tarnish his reputation in the months immediately following his death. Most people who still remember my father believe he was a shameless womanizer. I hate that she did that to him."

Brie put her hand over his and squeezed gently. "Maybe we can change their perception."

Sir discounted her suggestion. "People would rather believe scandalous lies than the truth."

"I don't believe that, Sir. I think people long to know the good around them. They've just been blindsided so many times that they assume the worst."

He snorted. "Well, it's too late to repair it now. Most people don't know who my father was, and those who do couldn't care less." He stared at the ceiling and sighed heavily. "Life goes on."

Brie laid her head on his chest. "Thank you for showing me his picture, Sir. It makes me feel closer to you."

He put his arm around her. "It was time."

She lifted her head. "Sir, would it be all right if we put his picture in the living room? It doesn't seem right to have him hidden in the closet when he was such an exceptional man."

Sir closed his eyes and didn't speak for several moments. "Brie, I still see visions of him dying when I look at this photo."

Brie kissed his chest and murmured, "When you are ready, then…"

Master Anderson's Influence

B rie woke up alone. That *never* happened with Sir. She scrambled out of bed and threw open the bedroom door. She was immediately assaulted by a savory aroma of onions, bacon, and garlic. Brie hurried to the kitchen, but stopped as soon as she saw him.

Sir was dressed in only his black sweatpants while he stirred a large pot with a wooden spoon. He looked so damn sexy standing there in the kitchen alone. She hesitated to disturb him, and slinked back to hide around the corner so she could still take in the charming sight.

He must have sensed her presence. Without looking in her direction, he instructed, "Come and sit down, téa."

She was naked and hoped she would not dampen her seat while she watched her handsome Master cook. "Good morning, Master."

Still stirring the pot, he explained, "I woke up this morning with the sudden urge to create my father's favorite meal. I know this does not qualify as a breakfast."

Brie smiled, more touched than she could express

that he had cooked such a personal dish for her. "I've had plenty of savory meals at Tono's, Sir, and actually have grown to appreciate more hearty meals in the morning."

He glanced back and smiled at her. "As fetching as you look sitting at my table naked, I need you to get a pair of bowls and two soup spoons."

She immediately popped out of her chair and gathered the needed items, along with napkins and glasses. She set the table and then placed the crocuses in the middle for an added touch.

Sir nodded his approval. "The dish is called *ribollita* and includes a host of vegetables, including carrots, cabbage, celery, and kale. But what makes it delicious is the pancetta." When she tilted her head, he handed her a small piece of round, bacon-like meat. "Taste."

She took a small bite. It was more delicate in flavor than bacon because instead of the smoked flavor, it tasted of Italian herbs. "Very nice, Sir."

"It's not just the meat, but the cannellini beans and sourdough bread that elevate it to favorite food status." Sir explained with a smirk, "I even added a small amount of tomato paste for color, but not enough to taint the dish." He went back to stirring the pot. "I thought you might like that."

Brie finished the last bite of pancetta and licked her fingers before answering. "I like it very much, Sir. Thank you."

He took the bowls from the table and ladled the thick stew into them. He brought them back to the table and added a generous sprinkling of parmesan cheese and a drizzle of olive oil, before sliding a bowl over to her with a look of satisfaction.

She took a deep sniff of the steamy mixture and smiled. "It smells heavenly, Sir."

He sat down and lifted his spoon, waiting for her to do the same. Together they spooned up healthy portions, and he cautioned her to blow on hers. She couldn't help smiling as they both took a bite.

The stew had the consistency of oatmeal, the bread having soaked up all the stock. The combination of the savory meat with onion and garlic gave the whole dish an Italian profile, but the soaked bread reminded her of a French dip, a favorite comfort food of hers.

She purred after she had finished her first bite. "Sir, I understand why this was your father's favorite meal. It's the best stew I've ever tasted. I could eat it morning, noon, and night."

"I'm pleased you approve," Sir replied, his eyes sparkling.

The two of them ate the meal in pleasant silence, savoring every morsel. She could almost imagine Alonzo standing beside them, smiling in satisfaction. Brie wondered if Sir could feel it too.

After breakfast was over, he beckoned her into his lap. She gratefully climbed into it and laid her head against his shoulder.

His masculine hands lightly stroked her soft skin. "Brie."

She smiled and looked up at him. "Yes, Sir?"

He gazed into her eyes and said nothing. Then Sir pressed her head against his chest again. "This was good," he finally stated.

Brie felt certain he had wanted to say something more, but she readily agreed with him. "Yes, it was the second best way I can imagine waking up." She glanced at him and blushed when she asked, "Do you think you could teach me how to cook it?"

He chuckled. "You? Hmm…"

She bit his bottom lip playfully.

Sir grabbed her face with both hands and kissed her soundly. "Yes, girl who can't cook. I will teach you." He lifted her off his lap and slapped her ass. "But not now. Clean up the kitchen and then ready yourself to visit Master Anderson."

Brie made quick work of the kitchen. She was thrilled at the prospect of seeing her old trainer again, mainly because she knew that Master Anderson was a good friend of Sir's. It would be beneficial for Sir to discuss his mother with someone who knew him well. However, she also liked the trainer on a personal level. Master Anderson had always been kind and respectful to Brie, even when he had held a bullwhip in his hand.

They arrived at his home before ten that morning. The trainer was out in the front yard, picking weeds. It was the last thing Brie would have imagined a Dom doing. Of course, he did it with his shirt off so that his thick arm muscles were properly displayed. She scanned the houses nearby and noticed several ladies 'watering their lawns'. Evidently, Master Anderson was doing his part to beautify the neighborhood.

The impressive trainer stood up and swept the dirt from his hands with an inviting smile on his face. "Well, if it isn't my old buddy, ex-Headmaster Davis, and his sidekick, Brie."

He grabbed Sir in a manly hug and slapped his back several times. Sir returned the gesture with more resounding thuds.

"Good to see you, Brad."

"Likewise."

Brie blushed when Master Anderson turned to grace her with his intense green stare. "May I?" he asked Sir.

"If you must."

Brie squealed as Master Anderson picked her up and twirled her around in the air several times. He set her back down, grinning. "Young Brie, it's always a pleasure to see you."

Sir shrugged. "It's something he used to do in college, but I thought he had outgrown that juvenile habit."

Master Anderson smiled charmingly, nodding at the neighbors. "It gives all the married women watching something to daydream about. I don't have the liberty to touch them, but that doesn't mean I can't tease them a little."

Sir grunted. "Looking to cause trouble, are you?"

"No, I just enjoy bringing a little spark to their lives. You should see how they gather when I practice my bullwhip out back."

Brie giggled. She could just imagine the stir he caused among the lady-folk.

"You're going to get yourself tarred and feathered if you aren't careful, Brad."

Master Anderson laughed. "It might surprise you to learn that a few husbands have asked for tips. Seems the woman here have developed a taste for the bite of a whip. Naturally, I steer them towards crops. Safer for everyone that way."

Brie piped up, "Maybe you should teach a class on the bullwhip. I know Tono's session on Kinbaku was very well received."

He smiled down at her. "Maybe I should, young Brie. Point well taken."

"How did you enjoy being an official trainer at the Center this time around?" Sir asked.

Master Anderson directed both of them towards the house. "It was an experience, Thane. The overall atmosphere has shifted under new leadership. There is no question that the rules are being adhered to, but...it lacks something vital since you left."

Sir slapped him on the back. "I think you just miss the ribbing we used to give each other after each session." He chuckled to himself. "I must say, it was agreeable working with you again."

Master Anderson opened the door for them and ushered them in. "So, Thane, what brings you here so soon after your return to the States?"

Sir did not answer him until they had all taken a seat in Master Anderson's study. Upon seeing it, Brie was reminded of her last visit here, the night she'd hosted the trainer's party—a night of many memorable encounters.

She settled down at Sir's feet, resting her head lightly on his thigh.

"I had an altercation with *her*."

He held such disdain in his voice that Master Anderson did not need to question to whom he was referring.

"When?"

"The beast befriended Brie while I was gone. I was met with her unpleasant presence upon our reunion."

"The nerve of the bitch!"

"You would not believe the lengths she went to. It's not only pathetic, but desperate. So desperate, it's given me insight into her motives."

"What could she possibly want? She took everything."

"I have to assume she is alone and destitute," he said coolly.

"But why come to you? I thought the woman was skilled at parting men from their money."

"I'm not certain what brought her to this point, nor do I care." Sir glanced at Brie with a look of regret. "But now Brie has to deal with the consequences of the unwanted reunion."

Master Anderson spoke with the candor of a good friend. "To be blunt, I am glad you have her with you. This is not something you should face alone." He stood up, walked to the expansive bookshelf lined with liquor bottles and poured both of them glasses of Scotch. "Have you spoken to your uncle about it?"

Sir shook his head as he answered, "No, not yet. Besides you and Nosaka, no one knows of her return. I think it's best to keep it that way, but I agree that he should be warned."

Brie had forgotten that Mr. Reynolds was related to Sir's mother. How would he react to the news? She couldn't imagine the kind old man being brother to such a spiteful woman.

"Yes—in fact, the sooner the better, Thane. He should not be surprised by her the way you were. You remember how it ended between them."

"Yes..." Sir said distractedly, as if he was remembering the event. "Unc felt as if he was to blame for what happened. Foolish on his part."

Master Anderson held up his glass. "No more foolish than you."

Sir snarled ominously as he took a drink. "Shut up."

"You know you came today because you needed someone to be honest."

"Don't be so sure."

Master Anderson finished his drink and grabbed Sir's glass without asking, filling it up with more Scotch.

When he handed it back, Sir stated, "You should know I don't care to drink before noon." Then he looked at Brie. "Would you like some, téa?"

His question did two things. It acknowledged that he cared about her well-being, but by calling her by her sub name, he was also informing her that she was there to observe and not participate in the conversation unless commanded.

Brie did not want the liquor to dull her response to him. "No, thank you, Master."

Master Anderson sat back down. "I thought a little Scotch was in order. It's not every day that Ruth Davis comes to call."

Sir shot up off the sofa and roared, "Do *not* use my father's surname with that woman!"

Brie was confused for a moment, until she realized that Sir's mother had even lied about her name. The woman had lied about everything…

Master Anderson got up and placed his hand on Sir's shoulder. "A mistake, my friend."

Sir exhaled angrily, but sat back down.

Master Anderson returned to his chair with a calm air about him. "How are you planning to handle it, Thane?"

"I am siccing my lawyer on her. He'll find out soon enough what's really going on." Sir directed Brie, "Don't let her get anywhere near you. The woman is toxic in every sense of the word." He looked back to Master Anderson. "The beast was able to finagle Brie's business card from her."

"I'm sorry, Master," Brie whispered.

"Téa, I do not fault you, but it illustrates the lengths to which she will go."

Master Anderson assured him, "I will keep an eye out for the beast. But after so many years, I'm not even sure I'll recognize her."

Sir laughed unkindly. "She probably went bankrupt because of her face. The whore looks the same—it's unnatural, like looking at the picture of Dorian Gray. She's made herself into a freak of nature in her frantic attempt to keep the only thing of value she has left—her looks."

"I honestly can't imagine her looking the same after all these years," Master Anderson mused.

"The only thing that gives her away is the gray in her hair. Gives her a cougar look, which must be advantageous to her somehow."

"I can see the value in keeping some of the gray. Imagine jumping into bed with what you thought was a young chick, but unwrapping an old woman."

Both men laughed, but Sir's expression quickly soured. "I've struggled all these years, knowing she was alive but my father was not. The only thing that kept me sane was the assurance I would never see her again."

Master Anderson put his glass down and said solemnly, "Thane, you never dealt with it. No matter what the future holds, I believe you will navigate your way through this and be a better man for it, when all is said and done."

Sir picked Brie up and pulled her close to him. "My sub seems determined to challenge me in this area, whether it's intentional or not."

Master Anderson picked up his glass again and raised it to them. "Then it's the perfect match, is it not?"

Sir kissed the top of Brie's head and then let her go, commanding, "Téa, go to the kitchen and whip up something for lunch. I would like to spend time with Master Anderson alone."

Brie bowed, thinking, *Oh, God. Whipping up 'something' for Master Anderson, the gourmet chef?* "My pleasure, Master."

The men exited through the back door, leaving Brie all alone in Master Anderson's house. She wished she could sneak over to the door to hear what they were discussing. Listening to these two Doms converse was fascinating, because with every exchange she learned a little more about Sir.

She glanced around the impressive kitchen. It was the kind of setup that belonged on a cooking show.

Although Sir's also had marble countertops and stainless steel appliances, Master Anderson had a ton of extra cooking tools that would make a chef's heart palpitate. However, they just confused Brie.

She decided to stick to the basics. There was no point in trying to impress either man, for Brie knew she would only end up embarrassing herself. Instead, she concentrated on what Sir liked, and what she could cook semi-decently. Brie checked through Master Anderson's refrigerator to make sure he had the needed items before she began.

Brie cooked the bacon in a pan first. It was one thing she was good at, having been given the task by her mother from an early age. Her mother didn't trust her with much in the kitchen, but bacon was one of Brie's specialties. She prided herself on getting it to that 'just crisp but not overcooked' stage.

Soon Master Anderson's house was filled with the delicious smell of bacon. While she let it rest on a paper towel, she set to work on the cheese. Normally she just used American, but Master Anderson did not have 'fake' cheese in his kitchen. Instead, she went with Gruyère, fontina, and for a personal touch a little Brie de Meaux. It would be a white grilled cheese, but that made it seem more gourmet to her.

The kitchen had the kind of grill you would find in a diner. It looked intimidating to operate, but Brie messed with the temperature until it seemed hot enough. She spread butter on the bread and placed the sandwiches on the heated grill. They sizzled pleasantly upon contact. Brie grabbed a spatula and watched the cheese intently as it slowly began to melt.

In her best cooking show voice, she announced, "You will find that the combination of cheeses will meld together to create the ooziest, most gooey grilled cheese you have ever eaten. Adding the bacon gives it a more savory flair, for those men of yours who need a little meat on their plates."

She lifted a corner of one sandwich and smiled. "You want to wait until you get a golden brown color. Too soon, and your grilled cheese will be unpleasantly mushy." She looked at the pretend camera. "Totally *not* delish!" She flipped the sandwich over. "If you wait too long, then you get the dreaded barbecued grilled cheese, and we ain't talking Memphis-style, people."

Brie set out three plates and grabbed a sprig of fresh parsley. Then she lovingly placed the sandwiches on the plates and stood back with a proud smile. "And that, my friends, is how you cook a killer grilled cheese!" She bowed gracefully, then turned to the pretend camera and ran her fingers across her throat. "Cut!"

She hurried to open the back door to let Sir know that lunch was ready, but stopped short when she saw the two men. Master Anderson was instructing Sir how to handle the bullwhip. Her knees almost gave out as she watched Sir swing the whip back and forth before hitting the bottom of the post with a loud snap.

Master Anderson shook his head and repositioned Sir's arm. This time, Sir stared at the post with intense concentration before swinging again. He lashed the post directly in the middle. It was as if Brie could feel the sting of it on her back, and she almost dropped from the impact.

Both men looked in her direction. Brie realized she must have made a noise and blushed. To cover it, she announced with a respectful bow, "Lunch is ready, Master." She hoped it wasn't obvious how much she was trembling.

"We'll join you in a minute, téa."

Brie bowed again and shut the door. She made her way back to the kitchen to finish setting the table, but her mind was not on her task. *Sir is practicing the bullwhip.*

He knew her feelings about the bullwhip. He had asked her the night she'd scened with Master Anderson at The Haven. It frightened her, the thought of being whipped again…

Maybe it was simply a way to relieve his stress. Men often bonded over physical activity. Typically it was over a game of basketball, but considering their kinky inclinations, chatting over a bullwhip seemed perfectly natural, right?

The men walked in, both sweaty from their workout. Brie looked at Sir through hooded eyes as he sat down. He winked at her before looking down at his plate. "I see you went with an American classic, téa."

Master Anderson pulled the bread apart to examine it more closely. "But with a uniquely Brie twist to it," he added with a smirk. He reassembled the sandwich and took a bite, announcing afterwards, "You went with a blend of three creamy cheeses. Good choice. The outside is nice and toasted, the cheese properly melted, but I can't say I care for the selection of meat. I think a slice of tomato would suffice."

Sir took his own bite. His face showed little expression as he chewed. After he had finished, he glanced at Master Anderson as he informed Brie, "Naturally, I disagree with the addition of tomato. I believe by replacing the bacon with pancetta you would have a fine sandwich, téa."

Brie wanted to burst with pride. Her first culinary success with Sir! He had eaten what she'd served him ever since she'd become his submissive, but this was her first real triumph. She wanted to squeal with happiness and struggled to keep quiet. It was only a grilled cheese sandwich, after all.

It seemed that Sir was more relaxed after his practice session with Master Anderson. He was more like himself during the meal, but insisted on leaving shortly after.

"I thank you for your time, Brad. As always, talking with you gives me a healthy perspective."

"Think nothing of it."

"Now you can go back to teasing the neighborhood."

Master Anderson grinned. "Think of the thrill you would cause if both of you joined me in weeding the front garden. Two bare-chested men and a little sex kitten in a miniskirt. I'm sure we could get the entire neighborhood out for the show."

Sir shook his head. "You need to get a permanent sub."

"Gardening has a calming effect, Thane. Maybe you should look into it."

Sir scoffed and walked out through the front door. "Come, téa."

Master Anderson said to Sir as he left, "Don't forget what I said about Wallace."

Sir stopped and turned to address him. "I'll set up a meeting tomorrow. It will be a relief to Marquis, who has been pushing for it since Brie's encounter with him at the Training Center. Personally, after yesterday's trouble I need to tie up those loose ends. The beast alone is enough for me to deal with."

"Good luck. Give me a call afterwards. In fact, why don't you drop by, and you can practice some more?"

Brie's eyes widened when Sir agreed. He was serious about learning the bullwhip! That could only mean one thing—he meant to use it on her. A cold chill ran through Brie, but an enticing shudder accompanied it. The knowledge that she was *his* and that this was an area he was going to push her in was…exhilarating.

The Wolf Howls

The meeting with Todd Wallace took place at The Haven. Faelan had refused to have it at the Training Center, stating that it should be on neutral ground.

Sir had been puzzled by his assertion that it was not neutral ground, but Brie understood. Both she and Faelan had been students at the Center. No matter how much experience they accumulated, they would always be pupils of the school.

The owner of the club had set aside a quiet room in the back for the meeting, away from the playful chaos. When they arrived, Sir turned to Brie. "At all times, be open and honest with him. If he sees the slightest hesitation, he will read it as you hiding your affections for him. Although Wallace is unusually talented, he remains emotionally stunted."

'The death of the young man in the car crash…" Brie said softly.

"Yes, it is the reason for his immaturity, but not an excuse to behave dishonorably."

"I will remember that, Sir."

"Look him in the eye."

"Yes, Sir."

Tension filled the air, but it immediately dissipated the moment Sir touched her, just before he guided her into the room. "You are an exceptional person, Brie. Beyond being a submissive, beyond your film talent, you are a kind soul," he said, brushing her cheek with his hand. "A true rarity."

Brie pressed her cheek against his hand, closing her eyes in contentment. "You make me a better woman." She opened her eyes and gazed into his. "I love you, Thane."

He returned her smile. "I love you." Sir kissed her then, their connection born of love and admiration.

When Brie entered the room, she knew with certainty that not only could she do this, but she could do it with the purity of love Tono had shown her. She noticed that there was only a single table with four chairs in the room. Faelan was seated directly in front of her, with Marquis Gray sitting on the right.

Faelan stared at her from across the room. Despite the situation and the people involved, she was irresistibly drawn to those deep blue eyes.

"Welcome," Marquis Gray said, directing Brie to the chair across from Faelan, and Sir to the one directly opposite him.

They all sat down in uncomfortable silence. But Brie followed Sir's orders and looked Faelan directly in the eye, despite her natural inclination to stare at her lap.

"Well, isn't this quaint? It's like I'm in jail. Here we have my lawyer, sitting next to me," Faelan said, pointing to Marquis Gray, "and there, you have the warden."

Brie smiled to herself at the comparison.

Marquis spoke up. "He has a few things to go over with you, Miss Bennett. Both Sir Davis and I will remain silent unless we can add clarification to the discussion."

Faelan looked down at a piece of paper in front of him and snarled. "No!" He swept the paper aside. "I am not going down a list." He stared at Brie. "You and I are going to have a genuine conversation, with no pretenses."

Brie noticed that Marquis discreetly slid the paper back over to him.

"That's acceptable to me, Mr. Wallace," she replied.

"To begin with, you will *not* call me Mr. Wallace. That just sounds wrong."

Brie looked in Sir's direction for guidance. He did not speak, but nodded slightly.

"Okay… Todd."

Faelan sat back in his chair and snorted. "That's only a slight improvement."

She wasn't willing to argue the point, so she forged ahead. "The reason we are here is to—"

"No, that's not how this is going to play out," he stated firmly as he took over. "As you know, I have lived in darkness most of my adult life. The guilt of killing someone has eaten at me like a cancer."

Brie replied compassionately, "But it was just an acciden—"

He held up his hand. "There's no point in continuing that line of thought, Brie. I've talked to a counselor and I'm not about to rehash it with you."

She looked down at her lap but immediately looked back up, realizing she was subconsciously falling into the submissive role with him.

"That day… The day you fell into my arms I finally saw a spark of hope. You were a light in the suffocating darkness consuming me." Faelan grinned at her. "I can't explain why, but there was an instant connection made I've never felt before." He leaned forward and asked her, "What did you feel that day?"

Brie took a deep breath before she began. Sir had instructed her to be honest, so she kept that her primary goal. "I was grateful that you saved me from a bad fall and I thought you had nice eyes. Honestly, I felt nothing more than that."

Faelan sat back and nodded. "When I saw you tied up later, while I was jogging on the beach, I almost lost it. I thought you were being kidnapped and raped."

Brie blushed. "That was an awkward moment for both of us." She looked upon Faelan with empathy. "But I appreciate that you were trying to help."

"I will never forget the sight of you, Brie. Knowing that you were naked under that robe when you came to the door. Seeing you caress the collar around your neck… The possessive way the Russian lorded over you." Faelan paused. "That was the beginning of a new life for me."

Brie interjected, "I didn't feel that way, Todd. In fact, I didn't realize who you were until the cops were about to leave."

"You felt no connection, not even then?"

She shook her head. "Not even when you formally

introduced yourself the next day. All I could think was that you were the last thing I needed."

He looked at her intently. "You needed a Dom, that's why I fell under the radar. As soon as I realized what you were, I understood what you required. Since that day, I have endeavored to become the man you needed."

Brie felt a twinge of guilt. "I never asked you to."

"You say that, but I know the first time we scened together you felt the connection, Brie. Don't deny it. Don't you dare deny it in front of these two men."

She gazed into his blue eyes, not shying away from her answer. "Yes, I admit it. You surprised me that day. I was impressed by you, despite my reservations."

"That's because I understand who you are, Brie. Yet, it's more than that. You and I are cut from the same cloth. We're both young and adventurous. We both hide an animal that no one else sees."

This time Brie looked away. It was true; there was a side of herself that only Faelan seemed to bring out. It was a side that was wild and dangerous.

He continued, "After our scene, with every interaction you were playful and inviting. Especially when I had to punish you and your two girlfriends."

It was embarrassing to have him bring that up in front of Sir. Brie shifted in her seat, remembering quite well the night he'd commanded she use her vibrator for a half hour without orgasming. It had been a long and frustrating night, which had only served to make her desire the young wolf more. "It was an unfair punishment," she responded.

His eyes sparkled mischievously. "I thought of you that night, Brie. Thought of your glistening, wet pussy struggling not to come because *I* commanded it."

Brie shivered under the power of his domineering confidence and broke their gaze again.

"Such descriptions are not necessary," Marquis Gray warned quietly.

"Brie," Sir said.

She forced herself to look into her Master's eyes, embarrassed by the feelings Faelan evoked in her—feelings she knew were obvious to both Sir and Marquis Gray.

"Remember what we talked about," he reminded her.

Brie bowed her head in response and turned back to face Faelan. "It was an order I completed because I was in training and it was my duty, Todd."

He smiled at her knowingly. "It drew you closer to me so that you were ready when I won you at the auction. There, you gave yourself over with no reservations. Do you remember that night? You opened up and released the animal that lay buried deep inside. That's when you finally understood, as I did, that we were meant for each other."

Brie's heart constricted. She knew her next words would wound him. "As much as I enjoyed our time together, I never loved you."

Faelan dismissed the unwanted truth. "You've said that before, but I still maintain you can't know that for certain. You and I were never given the chance to explore our feelings for each other because of the Headmaster." He gave a slight nod towards Sir without looking at him.

Brie smiled sadly. "I suppose you're right. You never had a chance because I love Sir. I have loved him from the very beginning."

Faelan growled. "Which is completely against school policy, I should point out. I'm sick and tired of being lectured by the trainers of this school about protocol when the very man who ran the Training Center desecrated it." He leaned forward and said in a low voice, "I know for a fact you chose him at the collaring ceremony because he manipulated you."

She closed her eyes, dreading sharing the hurtful truth with him. A truth even Sir did not know.

With renewed determination, she opened her eyes to face Faelan. "At the collaring ceremony, I planned to ask Tono to be my Master. If his father hadn't scorned the match, I would have become his submissive that night, not yours."

Faelan shook his head in disbelief.

Brie didn't even dare to glance at Sir when she continued, "It's true, Todd. Although I have lusted after you, I realized at the ceremony I could never partner with a man I did not love."

The room went deadly silent. "I don't believe you," he finally stated.

"I was always upfront with you about how I felt."

It was as if Faelan hadn't heard her. "How could you love that one-trick pony? It was painfully obvious to everyone but you that you wouldn't have been happy with Nosaka."

Brie's hackles went up. How dare he ridicule Tono

by calling him that? She took a deep breath, refusing to start an argument with Faelan. "You have no idea what you're talking about. At the collaring ceremony, I realized it could not work between us with his father being against the match. Which was a good thing, because it pushed me to do what my heart truly wanted." She glanced at Sir and smiled. "Sir is the only man whose collar I ever want to wear."

Faelan snarled and then turned on Sir. "Why the hell did you train me if you were planning to steal her away?"

Sir met his anger with an equal level of calm. "When you approached me about training as a Dom, I recognized your potential. Despite my better judgment, I took you under my wing because I understood your pain and knew this was a healthy direction for you to pursue. Unfortunately, I did not appreciate how immature you were, and am glad to hear you are getting professional help now."

"Is that supposed to be meant as an insult?" Faelan demanded.

"No. It's a simple fact that you cannot guide a submissive well if you are unable to control your own emotions."

Faelan threw back his head and laughed. "Oh, like you? What right do you have to tell me what to do? Answer me that, 'Headmaster'!" Faelan looked earnestly at Brie, reaching out for her across the table. "Did you catch what he just said? Your 'Master' admitted that he can't guide you properly. At least I'm doing something about it. It's not too late, Brie. Get out while you still can, in front of both of these men, so there's no question it came from you."

Brie took his outstretched hand and squeezed it. "Todd, I am content with my choice of Dom. I love Sir. Loving him makes me happy—far happier than I've ever been."

Faelan snarled. "It's not right! He's too old for you, *and* too arrogant."

She answered quietly, "'Arrogant' is a word I would use to describe you."

"Confidence, Brie. Not arrogance. I am confident we are good together and confident that we were meant for each other."

Brie smiled sadly. "You claim to love me. If that's true, then you should *want* me to be happy. I am happy, truly happy with Sir."

She saw him swallow hard, even though his confident expression never changed. "You've been brainwashed."

That flippant statement pissed Brie off. "Don't belittle my feelings like that. I love Thane Davis. You have to accept that."

"Brie, 'Headmaster' can have any girl he wants, but I *need* you."

She felt his desperation, but refused to give in to it. "As much as I care about you, Todd, I would never wear your collar."

His eyes narrowed. "So you will turn away my love without any thought or consideration."

"I know my own heart," Brie answered.

"And you're condemning me to a life without love?"

"No." An image of Mary instantly came to mind. "I

know of at least one person who cares about you, but you are oblivious to it."

His blue eyes flashed with vehement anger. "There is something you should know about me, Brie. I run either hot or cold. I am a passionate man and cannot be lukewarm like Nosaka. I will *not* be your 'friend' after this. If you tell me it's over, I will not acknowledge you when our paths cross again. For me, you will cease to exist."

His declaration hurt. The idea that Faelan would cut her out of his life completely had never occurred to Brie. "Does it have to end that way?" she asked, shocked.

"If I'm to keep my sanity, yes."

Brie looked at Marquis Gray, hoping he would impart some wisdom to Faelan, but he remained silent. She closed her eyes then, trying to keep back the tears that threatened to fall.

Faelan pleaded with her one last time. "Brie, I know you have feelings for me. Don't let this be the end of us. Don't."

There was no question what her answer must be. She opened her eyes and gazed into those beautiful ocean blues of his. "If that's how you want it to be, then I guess this is goodbye."

He stared at her as if he hadn't heard.

Marquis Gray spoke up. "Before we conclude this meeting, there are several things we need to go over."

Faelan's voice was hollow when he answered Marquis. "It is unnecessary. Everything listed there has just been taken care of."

He stood up slowly, as if in a daze, and left the room

without another word. The sound of the door closing made Brie's heart sink. Her bottom lip trembled, even though she willed herself to remain composed.

"I don't think the meeting could have gone any better," Marquis stated.

Brie nodded, even though she hated how it had ended. The pain in Faelan's eyes would haunt her forever.

"So what was on that list?" Sir asked Marquis Gray.

"We were going to set boundaries, but he's right. It is unnecessary now."

"Come here, Brie," Sir said with compassion. She melted into his embrace, needing his love to combat the ache in her heart. "You did what was required to set the boy free."

She nodded against his chest without looking up.

"Go ahead and cry, téa," he added softly.

The tears began to fall as she let out a deep sob. Sir held her tightly as she released the pain and guilt. When Brie was finally quiet again, she lifted her head and noticed that Marquis Gray had gone.

She felt bad and automatically apologized. "I'm sorry, Sir."

He smiled as he dried her tears. "For what? I know you are an emotional creature. It is something I value and choose to nurture."

As they prepared to leave the room, Brie stopped him and asked, "Sir, do you need me to clarify anything I said during the meeting?"

"Nothing you shared came as a surprise to me. Have you forgotten that you wear your heart on your sleeve, téa? It is something I find reassuring." He swept her hair back and kissed her tearstained cheek.

She laid her head against his broad chest and sighed. "That was hard, Sir. Harder than I imagined."

"Wallace's response was unusual, but in the end it may be the healthiest way for him to deal with it. I cannot fault him."

Brie nestled into Sir's embrace, feeling heartbroken for Faelan, but hoping that he was finally and truly free.

Release

Things became more settled after the meeting. Brie had met Faelan once already in public and, true to his word, he had not looked at or spoken to her. Although it was disconcerting for Brie, the new arrangement had freed Sir as well. Their relationship no longer carried the weight of Wallace's obsession, and he became more lighthearted as a consequence.

Brie knew something was afoot when she walked into the apartment and found a note beside a package. She picked it up and read:

> Buy the items on the list and make a rainbow roll for your Master.
>
> Leave it on the kitchen counter.
>
> Retire to the bedroom.

She smiled as she opened the package. Inside was a sushi-making kit with a cookbook. During her stay with Tono, he had instructed her in the basic skills of making sushi rolls, but she had no idea what a rainbow roll consisted of. Flipping through the colorful illustrations, she quickly found it and grinned. It looked like beautiful art. Thin slices of uncooked tuna, salmon and avocado were laid over a California roll. She quickly wrote down the ingredients and headed to the store.

Brie loved it when Sir gave her tasks like this— simple assignments that were completely vanilla in nature, but the outcome would be anything but. She shopped with a secretive smile on her lips, her sexy mission giving a sense of intrigue to the whole shopping experience.

When she returned home, she was surprised to find that the apartment was still silent. Brie speculated that Sir might be off with Master Anderson again. It inspired a vision of Sir cracking the bullwhip against the pole. Goosebumps covered her skin as she began working on the sushi roll.

She was determined to impress Sir with what she had learned under Tono's tutelage. Although her roll ended up being somewhat lopsided, the slices of raw fish and avocado covered up that fact. She stepped back to admire her handiwork.

Brie added a note of her own next to the plate: *I love you, Master.*

She skipped down the hallway to their bedroom, wondering what he had planned next for her.

The bed itself had been prepared for her with a new bedcover, golden handcuffs at the headboard and leg restraints at the bottom. On the pillow, she saw another note.

She felt butterflies in her stomach as she reached

over to pick it up. In his precise handwriting, she read:

Take the hood on the nightstand and put it next to the pillow.

Brie glanced at the nightstand and saw an unusual hood of silk. It was black with golden thread woven in a striking floral pattern. As beautiful as it was, a shiver ran down her spine as she put it beside the pillow and handcuffs.

Undress, leaving only your panties on.

Brie quickly stripped down, folding her clothes and laying them on the nightstand before climbing onto the bed to read her next order.

Lie on your back and restrain your legs so they are open wide for me.

Brie's heart beat fast as she bound her own legs for Master. It felt deliciously wicked. She lay back on the bed to read the final instruction.

Secure the hood around your head and cuff yourself to the bed.
Wait.

Brie was not a fan of hoods, but she dutifully put the silken material over her head and secured it loosely around her neck. Then she lifted her hands to the cuffs and tightened one around her left wrist. It was a bit of a struggle to secure the second, but she felt a sense of satisfaction when she heard the metal clink as it locked into place.

Now she was bound and ready for Master.

She lay there in a state of sexual arousal, waiting for him to claim her. The thin material of the hood allowed Brie to hear clearly. She caught the faint sound of movement in the kitchen and felt a thrill of excitement, knowing Sir had been in the apartment the whole time, silently observing her actions without her knowledge.

Brie waited with bated breath, the anticipation of his taking driving her wild with desire. When he finally entered the bedroom, she could *feel* his presence. Sir stood there for several moments in silence. She imagined him at the door, admiring her body, enjoying the scene he had created.

She found it alluring that he had chosen a different cologne to wear for the evening. A simple alteration of scent gave a whole new feel to their encounter.

She felt the bed shift when he sat down next to her. Brie gasped when he placed a piece of the cold sushi roll on her stomach. With thoughtful precision, he decorated her body with the meal she had prepared for him.

He stood back up, and a few seconds later she heard the click of a camera. Brie smiled under the hood, grateful she would be able to see his artwork later.

Sir returned to her and blew on her stomach before retrieving a piece of sushi with his mouth. Her heart fluttered at the contact.

How she loved being Sir's vessel...

Brie heard his low grunt of pleasure and wanted to

burst with pride. Another culinary success! Sir ate the piece he had placed on her nipple. The slow, sensuous way that he picked it up with his lips could make a girl come.

After he had swallowed the bite, his lips came back down and he sucked on her sensitive nipple. Brie wanted to press herself against his mouth, but stayed completely still so as to not disturb his feast. Sir continued his leisurely tasting, teasing her mercilessly as he went.

To Brie's mortification, partway through his meal her stomach gave a long, thunderous growl. Sir chuckled.

Her cheeks burned with embarrassment under the silk. *Why now?*

Sir undid the tie of the hood and uncovered her mouth. He kissed her on the lips before placing a piece of sushi into her mouth. Brie chewed it gratefully, hoping it would quiet her stomach's noisy protests.

She started to say, "Thank y—" but Sir put his finger to her lips, signifying that speaking was not allowed.

He kissed her again and gave her two more pieces before tying the hood back in place and finishing his meal. Her entire body was tingling by the time he was done.

Sir left the bed and she soon heard soft violin music fill the air. Brie wondered if it was a recording of his father's playing. The music was hauntingly beautiful and infused with raw emotion.

He returned to her side, running his hands over her body and leaving trails of fire wherever his fingers touched. They finally rested on her panties. He felt her mound beneath the wet lace and groaned.

Brie's pussy answered by pulsing against his hand. Sir gave a low growl as he literally ripped the panties from her body. Now she was completely exposed to her Master—tied, hooded, and cuffed for his pleasure.

Instead of moving between her legs and taking her like she'd expected, Sir lay beside Brie and played with her pussy. He began by teasing her clit first, getting her wet and desperate. Then he pushed two fingers inside and began caressing her G-spot.

Brie threw back her head and moaned as he made her loins contract in pleasure from the direct stimulation. He had played with her that way many times before, and her body responded by slowly building up to an intense orgasm.

That was when Sir changed tactics.

He repositioned himself and slipped his fingers back inside her velvety depths, this time pumping his hand at a vigorous rate. Brie was taken by surprise by the ferocity of it.

She moaned and began squirming as the slow buildup suddenly became an inferno of intensity. So intense, in fact, that she began to subconsciously fight against it.

Sir did not let up. His fingers rubbed against her G-spot at that alarming speed. Brie fought against her bonds harder, trying to get away. But without a means of escape, there was only one viable choice for her.

She commanded herself to let go. Brie consciously stilled her body and mind to accept his passionate invasion.

As soon as she did, a chill went through her as her

pussy contracted in violent pleasure, and a literal gush of wetness burst from her. Brie cried out in surprise at her watery release.

Sir's fingers left her and she heard him suck them as he tasted her wet climax. "Good girl. Let's try that again."

Brie was a slippery mess when he inserted his fingers back inside her still-quivering pussy and began pumping again. She arched her back to better allow the aggressive stimulation.

For a second time, she felt the intense buildup. "Oh, Master!" she screamed as a second powerful orgasm claimed her. Liquid flowed from her, splashing droplets everywhere.

"What is that?" she whispered from beneath the hood.

"It's your female ejaculation, my dear," he answered, kissing her through the silk. "And I must say, it tastes as sweet as rain."

He moved down to her pussy and started to eat her.

Brie was unsure if she could take further stimulation. "Please, Master. No."

"No is not an option, babygirl."

Sir swirled his tongue over her clit and growled when she tried to struggle. Brie instantly became still.

He licked her clit in a long, hard, rhythmic manner. Brie could imagine Sir's cock thrusting into her as it brushed against her clit, instead of his tongue. It didn't take long before her pussy began twitching with a need for sexual release.

This kind of climax was familiar and comforting to

her. She began mewing as his expert tongue brought her to the edge. She willingly gave in to the waves of pleasure, easily coming for her Master.

After the last wave had dissipated, he climbed on top of her and thrust his cock into her wet, overly sensitive pussy. The head of his shaft rubbed against her extremely swollen G-spot with concentrated abandon. This time she did not resist the stimulation, wanting to come around his cock.

Brie let out a loud, passionate scream when she washed his rigid shaft in yet another watery orgasm. Sir answered her by coming deep inside her pussy, the mixing of their essences complete.

"Sir... Sir..." Brie whimpered afterwards, overwhelmed by the experience and finding the darkness of the hood unsettling.

He immediately removed it and smiled down at her. "I'm right here, Brie."

She looked into his eyes in wonder. "I've never experienced anything like that."

"I was curious how you would respond to it. It requires a loss of control on a level that many women, even devoted subs, find difficult." He lifted himself off her and slid his hand down between her legs. "I love how slippery sweet you are. I have acquired a taste for you and will be demanding a sample whenever the urge strikes, téa."

Brie trembled at the thought.

Sir was releasing her from the restraints when the violin in the background began to play an achingly poignant melody. He stripped off the bedcover before lying down beside her and closing his eyes.

With pride in his voice, Sir confided, "My father used to play this song for me. He laid out all his emotions whenever he played, holding nothing back…"

It was so beautiful that a tear fell down Brie's cheek as she listened. "I can feel it, Sir. It's as if he is speaking to me through his violin."

Sir opened his eyes and gazed at her, finally nodding in response when tears welled up in his eyes.

Brie cuddled up next to him and they lay there, listening to his father speak through the song. The life and vitality Brie found in the touching piece belied the fact that his father was no longer living.

The ache in her heart grew when the song became lighthearted in nature. She could just imagine his father playing with Sir as a little boy. The love and passion in the music hinted at the beautiful relationship they must have had. Brie wasn't sure how Sir was able to listen to it without falling apart.

Once it returned to the hauntingly sad melody, she felt Sir's chest rise and fall in jerky movements and knew he was silently crying. She cried along with him, choking back the sobs as she soaked his shirt with her tears.

Brie instinctively knew there was healing to be gained from his painful release…

Wicked Game

Brie spent every waking hour working on her film the week before she was to present her documentary to Mr. Holloway. This was her last chance with the producer—either he would be satisfied with her changes, or he would withdraw his interest and she would have to start from square one, trying to find someone to take on her project.

There was no way Brie was going to let that happen.

Sir supported Brie in her work, demanding little from her as she poured her soul into the documentary. Not only did he take care of all the meals, but he handled her laundry. It made Brie extremely uncomfortable to see him take over tasks that were hers alone, but when she attempted to help, he reprimanded her harshly.

"Brie, you are disobeying a direct order. I do not want to see you do anything else until that documentary is complete. Do you understand me?"

Brie answered with a miserable, "Yes," frustrated that she was not only failing to care for her Master, but she had managed to disobey him in the process.

While she worked tirelessly on her project, Sir concentrated on coordinating his business in Russia while still meeting the needs of his American clientele. It kept him busy, but he still made time to visit Master Anderson on a daily basis.

It gave Brie nervous butterflies every time he left. The daily visits meant that Sir was taking his lessons seriously, and soon she would be feeling the sting of his newfound expertise.

Just before he was about to leave for another lesson, the doorbell rang. No one ever visited Sir without prior arrangement. Brie ran to the bedroom to throw something on as Sir went to answer the door.

She was worried it was bad news, but breathed a sigh of relief when she saw that it was Mr. Reynolds, Sir's uncle.

"Good to see you, Unc," Sir said, giving him a more heartfelt hug than normal before inviting him in. Mr. Reynolds smiled when he saw Brie, but his reserved manner let her know something was up. She immediately joined Sir on the couch.

"To what do I owe this unexpected surprise?" Sir asked pensively, picking up on Mr. Reynolds' unusual demeanor.

"I have been visited by..." He paused, as if unwilling to even say her name out loud in front of Sir.

"The beast?" Sir answered for him.

Mr. Reynolds let out a long, anguished sigh and simply nodded.

"What did she want?"

Mr. Reynolds sounded as if he was in pain when he replied, "I'm sorry, Thane."

Sir's voice became tense. "Sorry for what?"

"She's determined to see you."

Sir snarled. "You know I don't care what she wants. I refuse to speak to a woman who is dead to me."

Mr. Reynolds looked at him with an expression Brie could not read. "I would do anything to protect you, but she's crazy."

"Did she threaten you?" Sir asked with an eerie calmness, as if it had happened before.

"I'm not worried about us. Thane, I came to warn you. Ruth is determined to see you, no matter the cost."

"Did she say what she wants?"

"No. I tried to get it out of her to spare you, but she was closed-mouthed about it. Claimed it's a matter of life and death."

Sir growled angrily. "There is nothing she can say that I want to hear." He stood up and started pacing in front of the window that overlooked the city. "I want her out of my life, once and for all!"

Mr. Reynolds closed his eyes and groaned. "I know, Thane... I'm sorry for this. For all of it."

Sir snapped, "It is not your fault!" He recovered his inner calm before continuing, "This has no reflection on you. What is imperative is that we eliminate the problem before she can cause any further damage."

"How can I help?"

"All I ask is that you do not engage her again. Call the cops if you have to, but do not give her an audience. As long as we present a united front, all her conniving will be for naught."

Mr. Reynolds looked ill when he told Sir, "The reason I came straight over is that she threatened to head to the school next."

"The security staff has been apprised of the situation. They will be on the lookout for her. Do not concern yourself."

Mr. Reynolds said with confidence, "Thane, she will not go quietly."

"Fuck!" Sir began pacing again. Brie could feel the tension in the room rising to dangerous levels. "She will not ruin my life again. I will *not* allow it!"

"Sir, what are we going to do?" Brie asked, suddenly afraid for him.

"What am I going to do? I'll wait until I hear from the Center. It's possible she's bluffing and I refuse to react to idle threats."

No sooner had he spoken than his cell phone rang. Sir looked at the caller ID and frowned. "What is it?" he demanded when he answered the call. "Good God, Rachael. Call the police. I'll be there as soon as possible. Hopefully, she'll leave of her own accord."

Sir snapped the phone closed and asked his uncle, "Will you come with me?"

"Of course. No need to ask."

Sir turned to Brie. "You'll stay here. I do not want you getting involved with her again."

She insisted, "But Sir, my place is by your side."

"No, Brie. Work on your documentary while I am gone." Before she could protest, he added, "Obey me."

Brie held in her objection and watched both men leave the apartment in a rush. What could his mother have done to cause Sir to go against his better judgment?

She sat down with her computer and tried to edit her work, but she couldn't concentrate. She kept contemplating what was happening at the Center. What kind of mother would threaten her son? What was the woman capable of?

Although Brie appreciated Sir's protective nature, she wanted to be with him—*needed* to be with him.

She began pacing the apartment, contemplating driving down to the Center without his permission, until she heard a polite knock on the door.

Brie walked up to it hesitantly. She took a look through the peephole and saw a courier holding a manila envelope.

Brie asked him through the door, "Could you just leave it on the doorstep?"

"No, ma'am—I need a signature from the person it's addressed to. A Brianna Bennett."

She immediately thought of Mr. Holloway. "Could you slide it under the door?"

"That's highly unusual, ma'am."

"But could you do it anyway?"

The man grumbled as he bent down and forced the envelope under the gap at the bottom of the door. "The pen won't fit," he complained.

"Not a problem; I have a pen. Just a sec."

Brie picked up the manila envelope and looked it

over. It was big enough for legal documents and was addressed to her, although she noticed it did not have a return address on it. She went to the desk, signed her name on the slip for the courier and stuffed it back under the door.

He huffed as he bent down to pick it up. Brie peeked through the hole to watch him leave. Despite the man's obvious irritation, he tipped his hat before he left. "Thank you, ma'am."

Brie was pleased with the cautious way she had handled the exchange and eagerly tore open the manila envelope. Inside was another envelope, but it was addressed to Thane Davis. His name looked as if it had been written by a woman.

A feeling of nausea came over Brie and she had to sit down. The letter must have come from his mother...

Whatever was written in that letter might reveal the reason she was back. Brie was desperate to find out what it said, wanting to understand what kind of threat this woman posed to Sir.

Brie stared at the envelope for a long time, part of her wanting to destroy it and part of her wanting to secretly read it. There was no part of her that wanted to present the note unopened to Sir, but that was exactly what she decided to do.

When Sir returned home an hour later, he came alone. Although he looked cross, he was no longer irate.

Sir seemed relieved when he saw her sitting on the couch. "Whatever game she was playing, she ran off before I got there. Guess the threat of involving the police was enough."

Brie looked up at him, unable to hide her guilt.

"What is it, Brie?"

"A letter came while you were gone."

He looked at her apprehensively. "A letter?"

"I knew better than to open the door, Sir, but I let the courier slip it under. It was addressed to me. I thought it was from Mr. Holloway."

"But…"

"But when I opened it, there was a letter inside addressed to you." She glanced at the envelope on the table.

Sir looked at it in disgust and went to the kitchen. He came back and said, striking a match, "Whatever this is, it's gone now."

Just before the flame touched the paper, Brie blurted, "But Sir, maybe this will tell you her motive. You said yourself that you can't prepare to fight her until you know what it is."

Sir stopped and stared at the envelope, letting the match burn until it singed his fingers. He blew the match out and then set the letter back on the table.

He sat down next to Brie. "The fact it's here tells me two things. One, she knows where I live and two, she knows that you live here with me."

"I shouldn't have signed for the letter, Sir. I'm sorry." Brie bowed her head, feeling as if she had betrayed his trust.

"It doesn't matter. The only thing she learned from this little stunt is that you are an extremely trusting individual." Sir sighed, glancing at the letter again. "Either this will tell me the real reason she wants contact and it will infuriate me, or this is a clever lie she's concocted, which will infuriate me even more." Sir rubbed his chin, trying to decide if he wanted to open Pandora's box.

Finally, he picked it up and ripped the envelope open. He unfolded the letter and glanced at it before throwing it down. "Bullshit!"

Sir stormed out of the room. Brie hesitantly picked up the note to read it, and was shocked to see there were only five words.

I am dying of cancer.

Brie couldn't believe it. She ran to the bedroom to comfort Sir, but he was still in an uncontrollable rage. When she entered the room, he shouted at her, "That bitch does not have cancer any more than I do!" His laughter was low and angry. "Oh, but isn't she clever?"

"But what if it is true, Sir?"

He replied coldly, "I wouldn't care. She should know that. This is her clever way of garnering other people's sympathies. Look at the poor beast, dying of cancer while her son stands back and does nothing to help. Well, that's exactly what I plan to do. She can rot in hell. In fact, I would prefer it."

Brie was taken aback by his wrath.

Sir looked at her and snarled. "This is how she does it. She pits us against each other. She expects me to begin resenting you for giving me the letter, and you to be horrified that I would react to such news with indifference."

Brie crossed the room and stood beside him, stating her support in words as well as with her proximity. "There is nothing she can do to tear me away from you, Sir. I understand your righteous anger towards her and I believe you when you say that she's lying. I stand behind you and support you, Sir."

"No, Brie." He pulled her into his embrace. "You stand *beside* me."

She wrapped her arms around him. "Nothing can separate a condor from its mate, Sir."

He lifted her chin and smiled for the first time that night. "Brie, that is the only truth I need. You are a wise little sub."

She cocked her head. "*Wise*, Sir? Aren't I far too young to be described as wise?"

His spontaneous laughter was music to her ears. It delighted her heart to hear it.

Believe

B rie couldn't stop the buzzing in her ears. After weeks of shooting and retooling her documentary, her time had finally come. She bit her lip and closed her eyes, trying to rein her nerves in.

"Brie, what's wrong?" Sir asked.

He'd insisted on being with her as she waited to be called in, although he would not be present during the meeting itself. Sir felt it was important this was her success, and hers alone.

"Sir, I've never felt like this before. I think I'm going to faint, I'm so nervous."

He put his hand on her knee and gazed into her eyes, imparting his confidence. "You will not let your fears get the best of you."

She nodded, needing to hear his reassuring words.

"You have reworked the film to his specifications while remaining true to your vision. The work is better for it. However, if Mr. Holloway chooses to turn it down it will be his loss, for you *will* find someone to produce it."

Brie took a deep breath and smiled. "Yes, you're right, Sir. Someone will pick up my film if Mr. Holloway does not. This film is a winner—I can feel it in my bones."

"Hold onto that truth and do not let your nerves control you. Be self-assured without being arrogant and you will do well."

That extra shot of confidence was all she needed. "Thank you, S—"

The receptionist interrupted their conversation. "Mr. Holloway will see you now."

Sir stood up with Brie and gave her a quick kiss before letting her go. "Knock him dead, Brie."

She let out a nervous sigh and then shook her head. *No! My nerves are not going to control the moment.* Brie consciously released the tension and stood up straight, her chest out, her head at a respectful angle.

"That's my girl," Sir commented as she walked away.

Everything was perfect until she greeted Mr. Holloway and he barked an order to sit down. The inflection in his voice let her know the man was on edge and irritable. Not at all what she needed for her big moment.

Brie held out her hand and shook his. "Thank you for seeing me again, Mr. Holloway." To ease the tension in the room, she started off the conversation with a compliment. "As you know, sir, I admire your expertise and took your suggestions to heart as I reworked this film. I trust you will be as impressed with the changes as I am."

"I'll be the judge of that," the producer grumbled, grabbing the disk from her hand. He slid it into the player, then sat back in his chair, closing his eyes as if he couldn't be bothered to watch it.

Brie swallowed hard. It was one thing to be turned down because her work legitimately sucked, but it was quite another to lose out on her chance because the producer was upset about something she had no control over.

The lively music of the introduction started up. Brie had chosen something that would instantly grab the viewer's attention. She smiled, knowing the hard bass and driving beat were impossible to ignore.

Mr. Holloway opened his eyes a crack and watched as the opening credits showcased the three girls and the two trainers she'd interviewed. He sat up and took notice when a short teaser clip of the flogging scene flashed onto the screen.

Brie silently cheered, even though it still remained to be seen if she could keep his attention throughout the entire film, especially since it was twenty minutes longer with the additional scenes.

Believe…

Images of Sir, Tono and Marquis Gray came to mind. Brie turned her attention back to the screen and smiled as she watched her beloved film unfold.

Sure, Mr. Holloway might have a few questions or suggestions, but damn, the film was not only hot, but informative and riveting. Mary's part especially had taken on a life of its own. It was easy to see the vulnerability in her mannerisms and hear it in her voice as she talked about the effects of her abuse. However, Brie had assured Mary that she would not come off as a victim in the film. It had been Brie's mission to show how strong and courageous she was, despite her abusive past. Mary was not a person to be pitied. No, she was an inspiration.

Although Mr. Holloway watched the film with no emotion evident on his face, Brie did notice his keen interest when Marquis' scene with Lea came up. Even now, having seen it at least fifty times while editing, Brie felt the sexual stirrings that watching Marquis' masterful skill evoked.

When the scene was over, Mr. Holloway glanced over at her and stated, "That was powerful."

Brie hid her pride with a humble nod.

He did not speak for the rest of the film, but he did watch it in its entirety, then shut off the machine as soon as the ending credits began.

Mr. Holloway folded his arms and settled back in his chair. "What do you think of the film, Miss Bennett?"

Brie decided to be completely honest. "It is my masterpiece. The film explores the forbidden world of BDSM, but in a way that is not intimidating to the average viewer or irreverent to the lifestyle. I was pleased with the additions you requested because it gives the film a more emotional hook, without being simpering or demeaning."

He chuckled. "I especially enjoyed the added flogging scene. How did you manage to get permission from Coen to do that?"

Brie smiled. "Mr. Holloway, the staff at the Center stand behind what they do. I believe they are committed to giving an accurate picture of what submission can look like."

She was surprised that he frowned. Everything had appeared to be going well, but he definitely did not look happy and she felt the air leave her lungs.

"This has been a shitty week. No, the reality is that the last two months have been shitty. The last thing I wanted today was to like your work. I don't need the hassle. In truth, all I want to do is take a long vacation and forget the last few months ever happened. But it doesn't look like that's going to happen now."

Brie was finally able to breathe again. "I'm pleased to hear that, Mr. Holloway."

"I bet you are," he snarled, as if she had wronged him by creating quality work. "I'll show this around to a couple of my friends and get back to you next week. Looks like I'll be scrapping my last project in lieu of this one."

Brie stood up and gave him a firm handshake. "That is excellent news. I look forward to hearing from you."

She started towards the door, hardly feeling the floor beneath her feet.

"Oh, Miss Bennett. I highly suggest you take a vacation within the next couple of days. You won't have any downtime once the ball starts rolling."

"I'll keep that in mind, Mr. Holloway. Thank you."

"I'm serious—tell Davis he'd better set it up now, because I won't tolerate complaints later on that he never has time with his sub."

"I'll be sure to inform him, sir."

"Good." He waved her off as he picked up the phone and growled at his receptionist, "Get in here, damn it. We've got to revamp the whole fucking schedule…"

Brie shut the door behind her and walked towards Sir with a grin she could not hide. His confident smile greeted her. "I take it that it went well?"

"Yes, Sir."

"How well?"

"He said you should set up a vacation this week because there won't be any breaks in the foreseeable future."

His eyes lit up. "You did it!"

"I did it, Sir."

His warm laughter filled the office. "My babygirl, a famous filmmaker."

"Not yet, Sir, but soon."

He kissed her, still smiling when their lips met. "I think I will take the good producer at his word and arrange a quick trip. There is one place in particular we need to go," he informed her, as he rested his hand on the small of her back and guided her down the hallway.

"Where's that, Sir?" Brie had expected he would say Russia, but what came out of his mouth completely surprised her.

"We need to revisit Nebraska."

Brie nearly tripped over her feet. "Nebraska, Sir?"

"Something this important must be done in person."

In one fell swoop, he had sucked away all the joy she had previously felt. Speaking with her parents was going to be an exceedingly difficult conversation. "Very well, Sir."

"Take heart, little sub. I have someplace else in mind afterwards. A place I haven't been to in years."

Now her interest was piqued. "Where's that, Sir?"

"That, téa, shall remain my secret. I know how you cherish surprises."

Brie groaned. She couldn't stand not knowing and decided to probe with little questions. "Does it require a passport, Sir?"

"I will not answer any questions on the subject," he replied. But once they had left the building, Sir lifted her up and slung her over his shoulder, slapping her hard on the butt.

Brie squealed, trying to wiggle out of his arms. "What was that for, Sir?"

"That was your congratulations spanking."

Her attitude immediately changed. "Oh, well then, I'd like another, Sir."

"Too bad, my dear. You must wait." He set her down with a smirk.

"You are a cruel Master." She pouted as a group of businesswomen hurried by, staring at them reproachfully.

He leaned down and winked at one of them when he answered her. "Sometimes you must be cruel to be kind."

Brie took his hand and wove her fingers between his. "To be honest, Sir, I enjoy your cruel ways."

His eyes took on a mischievous glint as he squeezed her hand and walked her into an alley. "I suddenly have a craving for you, babygirl."

Brie's loins tingled as she followed him. She glanced back, noting the people walking on the sidewalk less than fifteen yards away.

"Panties off."

Her heart beat wildly as she stepped out of her panties and handed them to him. He slipped the thong into his jacket before pushing her against the brick wall. "I want to taste you," he growled huskily as he slipped his hand up her skirt.

Brie leaned her head back against the wall and let out a quiet moan as his fingers began caressing her pussy.

"That's it, téa. Relax as I finger-fuck you in broad daylight."

She peeked at the crowds walking by, aroused by the wickedness of what the two of them were doing.

Brie had to hold back her cry when his fingers slipped in and he began caressing her G-spot. "Let go," he whispered hoarsely as he forced her orgasm with his powerful hand.

She held nothing back, embracing the strange sensation as her body tensed and eventually released in a burst of intense pleasure. "Good girl," he praised as he knelt down and tasted her dripping wet pussy. His groan was a total turn-on.

She looked up at the patch of sky between buildings as Master continued to tease her clit with his tongue. Suddenly, she got an uneasy feeling and turned her head to see that an older gentleman had stopped in the alleyway to watch.

"Sir…"

Her Master gave her one last swirl of his tongue and then stood up, adjusting her skirt before wiping his mouth with relish. He leaned in and said lustfully, "Delicious," before taking her hand and escorting Brie past the voyeur. Sir didn't even glance in his direction, as if what they had done was a common occurrence that required no explanation.

The two of them continued down the bustling street hand in hand, like any vanilla couple in love.

Brie looked up at Sir, unsure if the happiness she felt could ever be topped. Her film was going to be seen all over the world and her Master loved her.

Could life get any better than this?

Challenge at The Haven

To celebrate her documentary, Sir took Brie to The Haven that night. It was hard not to tell everyone why she was so happy, but she'd promised Sir she would keep her recent success under wraps until she'd had a chance to talk to her parents. Sir insisted that they do it in person. Brie knew the discussion would not go well, so she buried it in the back of her mind and embraced the festivities and kinkiness of The Haven.

She saw that Tono was in the middle of a sensuous scene in one of the largest alcoves. There were a considerable group of Kinbaku enthusiasts watching his precision and skill. Brie stopped to admire his artful work.

The Asian Dom's hands glided over the sub as he finished adjusting his knots before lifting the girl into the air. Brie heard a woman beside her gasp and knew she was imagining herself in Tono's ropes, flying under his power. It was a common fantasy many of the subs shared.

Brie looked again and realized that she recognized

the submissive being suspended. It was Candy, the girl she had met on the light rail months ago—the one to whom she had given Sir's Submissive Training card. The look of ecstasy on the girl's face contrasted starkly with what Brie remembered from their first encounter. At the time, Candy had been in the service of an abusive wannabe Dom. She'd had the look of the worn and beaten, but to see her now one would never know it was even the same person.

Brie smiled to herself, glad she had made the sacrifice of the card when she'd felt the urging. As much as she had wanted to keep it as a memento, it was worth the joy she was experiencing right now at seeing Candy so happy and fulfilled.

Tono turned to secure a last tie and noticed Brie in the audience. He gave her a slight nod and then continued with his scene, whispering to Candy. The girl moaned in pleasure when his hand rested near her mound. He was the master of incidental touches— simple contact that could drive a girl wild.

Brie turned to say something to Sir, but he was no longer by her side. She moved through the crowd, anxious to find him. She tripped on a crop left carelessly on the floor and collided face first with a muscular chest. Brie looked up and was shocked to see Faelan staring at her. He was equally thrown off by the unexpected impact.

His blue eyes held her mesmerized for a brief moment before he pushed away from her and grabbed the woman beside him. He fisted the blonde's hair and pulled her head back to kiss her deeply.

Mary's surprised whimper shocked Brie even more than running into Faelan had. The two kissed long and passionately before Faelan broke the embrace. "Do you want to scene with me?"

Blonde Nemesis' eyes sparkled with expectation. "What kind of scene?"

"A little knife play," he suggested lustfully.

"I'm in."

"Good. I plan to play rough tonight." He escorted Mary through the crowd, leaving Brie behind without any acknowledgement. It was strange to be treated in such a bizarre manner, but Faelan had warned her that she would no longer exist in his world after she'd chosen Sir over him.

Brie could tell Mary was happy to play his impromptu sub in a scene, but it worried her. Brie was afraid Faelan was only using her. The fact was, Mary genuinely loved the guy and deserved much better than that.

Scanning the crowds, Brie was even more anxious to find Sir after her unexpected encounter. She finally spotted him on the other side of the large common area, engaged in conversation with Master Anderson. She started towards the two, but was stopped by her former trainer, Ms. Clark.

"What are you doing in the club alone?" Ms. Clark demanded.

Brie glanced down to avoid looking her in the eyes as she tried to respectfully move past her. "I'm not alone, Mistress. I'm trying to rejoin my Master."

Ms. Clark put her hand on Brie's shoulder and squeezed her sharp fingernails into her flesh. "Don't be flippant with me, sub," she snapped.

This time Brie looked her straight in the eye. "I am not being flippant, Ms. Clark." She tried to twist out of her grasp, but the Domme's hold was too tight.

Ms. Clark's eyes narrowed. "I have half a mind to take you in the back and teach you respect, Miss Bennett."

"Get your hand off my sub."

Ms. Clark instantly obeyed and addressed Sir. "I didn't realize you were here, Sir Davis. I was simply trying to protect your property."

"Touching my sub is never an option, Samantha. I believe *you* are the one who needs the lesson in respect."

"I'm certain you missed the exchange between Wallace and your sub just a minute ago."

"No, I did not."

"Then you understand my concern."

"No." Sir glanced at Brie. "Join Master Anderson."

"Yes, Master." Brie hurried to Master Anderson's side, wishing she had eyes in the back of her head. What had Ms. Clark been thinking? Nobody touched another Dom's sub without permission, not even trainers.

When Brie reached Master Anderson, she turned around to see Sir had one hand wrapped around Ms. Clark's wrist to prevent her from leaving as he spoke to her. The look on the Domme's face announced her discomfort. Obviously, whatever he was saying was upsetting to her.

The Domme tried to speak several times, but Sir interrupted and continued his lecture. It pleased Brie to see it. Someone needed to put that arrogant woman in her place.

The trainer shook her head violently, but it wasn't until she nodded that Sir let her go.

Sir came to Brie and announced, "Ms. Clark has something to share with you. Follow me."

Brie looked up at Master Anderson, who looked visibly troubled. His discomfort alarmed her.

She followed Sir and Ms. Clark. The Domme marched ahead of her angrily, clicking the studded heels of her thigh-high boots. Brie couldn't help focusing on the pointed heels, noting that they looked potentially lethal.

Ms. Clark headed to a private room with comfortable seating. She refused to sit, but gestured Brie towards a chair. Brie looked to Sir, who nodded his approval. She sat down hesitantly, curious about what was about to transpire.

"Go ahead, Samantha. Explain your past with Rytsar and how that has caused your odd fascination with my sub."

"I am not fascinated by your sub," Ms. Clark protested indignantly.

"In all the years I have known you, I have never seen you behave this erratically with a submissive before."

"I'll be damned if I am going to open up about my past in front of a student, Sir Davis."

"Ah, but she is no longer a student. Miss Bennett is now a respected and collared sub. You seem to forget that whenever she's around."

The Domme looked at Sir and pleaded, "Don't make me do this."

"You brought it upon yourself." He addressed Brie before leaving the room. "See me afterwards. I'll be practicing with Master Anderson in the whipping area."

Brie let out a barely audible gasp as her pussy contracted in fear. She found her voice and replied dutifully, "My pleasure, Master."

When he shut the door, Brie had to control the urge to run to it and fling it back open. The resentment radiating from Ms. Clark could kill a girl.

The Mistress sat down and crossed her legs, showing off the pointy, metal-studded tips of her lethal heels. It felt like an unspoken threat to Brie. She took heed and looked to the floor, not wanting to piss the Domme off.

"If this must happen, then we will make it short. Despite what your Master said, I am not fascinated by you in the least. But you already know that." She paused, then added menacingly, "Don't you?"

Brie nodded with her head down. There was no way she would be foolish enough to disagree with the woman.

Ms. Clark grumbled at the ceiling, "God, I can't believe he's making me do this!"

It was arousing to know that Sir had that kind of power over the Domme.

"I knew Sir Davis in college. I met Rytsar Durov through him. There was chemistry. Only barrier—he is a Dominant and so am I. It makes for a difficult partnering."

Ms. Clark seemed to be waiting for Brie to respond, so she said quietly, "I can only imagine, Mistress."

The trainer snorted angrily. "I was confident in my

role as a Dominatrix and I was young…" Her voice trailed off for a moment. "I made a critical mistake one night." The room filled with the woman's rising anxiety.

Was Ms. Clark going to cry?

But Brie's former trainer cleared her throat and finished with a simple statement. "Needless to say, it ended my chances with him." She sighed as if she was relieved her short speech was over.

Brie dared to look up and ask, "But what does that have to do with me?"

Ms. Clark's face contorted in revulsion. "When Sir Davis announced that he was inviting Rytsar to the first auction, I couldn't wait to see what he would do with someone so inexperienced and disobedient. But something happened that night." She gave Brie a death glare. "What did he see in *you*? You're nothing special! You're a failure as a submissive and yet you had him wrapped around your finger—the renowned Rytsar. You had them all eating out of your hand. It was unfathomable to me!"

Ms. Clark got up and stood over Brie, her animosity hitting Brie like palpable waves. Brie trembled under the weight of it. "If you ever tell anyone what I've shared here, I will permanently hurt you. I don't care about the consequences. Do you understand?"

Brie had to swallow down her fear to answer. "Yes, Mistress."

"So run along to your Master, you worthless cunt."

Brie got up and made a beeline towards the door.

Ms. Clark laughed behind her. "Maybe this was cathartic for me after all. I will have to thank Sir Davis."

Brie's heart was racing as she made her way back to Sir. She tried to act calm, although her interaction with Ms. Clark had been both terrifying and enlightening.

"Did she explain it to your satisfaction, Brie?"

She nodded, wanting desperately to enclose herself in his protective embrace. "I understand now, Sir. Thank you."

Ms. Clark sauntered up behind Brie. "Miss Bennett proved to be an apt listener. It actually feels good to get that off my chest." Her red lips curled up into a dangerous smile.

"You will not mistreat my sub again, Samantha." Sir lowered his voice so passersby would not overhear. "I tell you this as a friend. We all assumed once Miss Bennett finished training, you would return to your professional demeanor. That has not been the case. Should you continue to struggle in this area, I will be obligated to advise Headmaster Coen to rethink your tenure."

Ms. Clark raised her head proudly. "I assure you that is unnecessary."

"I'm aware that Miss Bennett challenges you. Frankly, she seems to have that effect on people. But that in no way excuses your appalling behavior. Now apologize to my sub. It is apparent you upset her during your *talk*."

Ms. Clark rolled her head from side to side, cracking her neck before replying. "As you wish, Sir Davis."

Again Brie felt a surge of excitement at knowing that her Master held that kind of power over the Domme.

Ms. Clark turned to Brie. "I apologize for being blunt."

Sir immediately corrected her. "Being blunt is acceptable, and something that would not have upset her." Brie loved that Sir knew her so well.

Ms. Clark insisted, "I needed to be clear that speaking about what I shared is not acceptable."

Sir's eyes narrowed. "It was unnecessary to threaten my sub, Samantha. A simple, 'You are not allowed to share this' would have sufficed. Brie is obedient."

Ms. Clark opened her mouth to protest, but Sir stopped her. "The fact she looks you in the eye on occasion does not reflect on her character as a person. She would honor your request without question."

The Domme clamped her mouth shut and glared at Brie. She took a deep breath and forced out the words. "I apologize for not respecting you as a sub, Miss Bennett."

"Thank you, Ms. Clark," Brie answered, lowering her eyes and bowing slightly. She understood the will it took for the Domme to humble herself like that. The level of respect Ms. Clark had for her Master was clear.

The Domme's smile returned as she spoke to Sir. "After this little episode, I plan to speak with your friend when he comes to visit again. I believe a conversation between us is long overdue."

"That would not be wise, Samantha. Let sleeping dogs lie," Sir warned.

"Your wisdom only goes so far, Sir Davis. There are times when a person must take a risk and become master of her own fate."

"I will not protect you again if it comes to that. You are too old to play the fool."

Ms. Clark crinkled her nose. "Too old? I'm just hitting my prime."

The Mistress strode off as if she were queen of the world. Brie observed two submissives fall in line after her. What Lea had said was true. Ms. Clark could have anyone she desired—all except the one man she wanted.

"Are you ready?" Master Anderson asked behind her.

Brie turned and her knees gave way when she saw the large bullwhip in his hand. Sir supported her and said with a chuckle, "No need to worry, little sub. There will be no blood tonight."

"Unless your Master screws up," Master Anderson joked.

"If I do not do well tonight, it reflects solely on you, *Master* Anderson."

"A teacher can only do so much," he replied, letting his bullwhip unwind, accentuating its dangerous length.

She watched with morbid fascination as Sir pulled a black bullwhip with a blood-red tip out of his bag. It made a slapping sound as it unfurled to the floor. She looked up at him nervously.

"Are you scared, téa?"

She nodded.

"Does it turn you on?"

She blushed when she confessed, "Only because it's you, Sir."

"I may not be a sadist, but I do enjoy challenging you, little sub. This will be a test for me as well." He ran his fingers between her trembling legs. "Yes, that is exactly the wetness I was striving for. Shall we begin?"

Sir escorted her to the chains and commanded her to undress fully and stand on the red 'X'. It felt a little like déjà vu as Sir put her small wrist above her head, strapping the cuff into place.

Brie's nipples hardened in fearful expectancy when he took her other wrist and secured it. She could hear the crowd gathering. Everyone enjoyed watching Master Anderson's expertise with the bullwhip.

As both men removed their shirts, Master Anderson informed the audience, "Tonight is simply a practice session. Sir Davis has been working with a fence pole for several weeks. Now it is time to practice on human flesh."

Brie could hear the excited chatter amongst the crowd. She suspected some of them *hoped* to see blood tonight.

Sir's hands ran over her body as he readied her for the experience. Whereas Rytsar had enjoyed her fear, Sir dispelled it. He tied up her hair and then kissed the nape of her neck. This was not a session meant to frighten; this was an extension of his sensual skills using the bite of a whip.

She held her breath when he pulled away from her, the fear sinking in. Brie's heart began racing as he positioned himself behind her. The smell of the ocean that was unique to this particular alcove in the Haven helped to calm her nerves. She'd never fully appreciated how different scents could prove valuable to a sub during a scene until now. Brie focused on the smell and immediate sensations, forcing back her fears of what was yet to come.

Master Anderson instructed Sir. "Keep your stance in mind. We'll start off light. Watch me first."

She imagined him winding up and then felt the light lick of Master Anderson's whip on her back. She smiled. It was pleasurable. Brie had forgotten how gentle the bullwhip could be, and she purred with pleasure.

Sir warmed up before giving Brie her first taste of his whip. The waiting made it that much more arousing and frightening.

"Are you ready, téa?"

"Yes, Master."

The light caress of her Master's whip took the experience to a whole new level. Brie moaned in satisfaction.

He continued to warm her skin with gentle strokes from his bullwhip, making the encounter delicious, not distressing. The control Sir showed was a testament to the amount of time he'd practiced.

"Now that her skin is prepared, it's time to increase the sensation," Master Anderson stated.

Brie forced herself to stay relaxed as she waited for Master Anderson to take his stance. He described his actions to Sir as he caressed her back with a more demanding stroke. It was strong enough to take her breath away.

She took a quick glance behind her and noticed that a larger crowd had gathered as Sir stepped into position behind her. Brie closed her eyes. There was no fear, only anticipation as she waited for her Master's stroke.

But Brie cried out in surprise and pain when the end of his whip made contact. It was much harder than Master Anderson's. She heard Sir mutter under his breath, "Fuck!"

"To be expected, all part of the learning process. You flicked your wrist at the end," Master Anderson explained. "Try again, but be conscious of that."

Brie did not realize she had tensed until Master Anderson commanded, "Relax, Brie."

She took a deep breath and let it out slowly. The chains clinked above her as she twisted in place. The movement helped release some of the tension, so she stilled herself for the next stroke.

"That's my good girl," Sir praised.

Brie trusted Sir completely, honored to be his first. Despite his extensive experience and the numerous subs he had trained, this was something exclusive—shared only between them. It pleased her to serve him in this way, the two of them a team as he learned to control the bullwhip.

Sir took his time before taking his next swing. Brie gasped at the challenge it provided, but it was not as overwhelming as the first had been.

"Color, téa?"

"Green, Master."

He grunted in satisfaction and began to take her into flight as he stimulated her back with well-placed strokes. Brie moaned in her chains as she began to lose herself to the sensation. Brie could sense the crowd, and it enhanced her experience. Their excitement played into hers. It was a glorious feeling...

Eventually, the rhythmic contact stopped. Brie swayed dreamily in the chains, ready to be released by her Master, hoping he would take her.

"I suggest you give her one more with bite before we end the session," Master Anderson advised Sir. Brie's heart skipped a beat as he explained, "It will do two things. For you, it will let you navigate the force required for a harder stroke that does not cause damage. For your sub, there is an erotic allure to experiencing the fierceness of the bite you can deliver. Every time you caress her with the whip, no matter how lightly, her pussy will drip because she knows it's your choice not to strike her harder."

Brie shivered in her chains. Although she agreed with Master Anderson, she did *not* want to feel the harsh bite again. Still flying on her sub high, she was unable to hold back the tears rolling down her cheeks.

Master Anderson demonstrated the motion it took to deliver a welt-worthy strike in the air first. Brie jumped each time she heard the crack of the whip beside her.

"Are you ready, sub?" Master Anderson finally asked, preparing her for his more forceful strike.

Brie understood that this was necessary to help hone Sir's skills. Despite her fears, she forced herself to answer with confidence through her tears, "Yes, Master Anderson."

He did not wait. With a quick and sure stroke, the tail of the whip cut across her back. Even though she had faced the biting power of his whip before, Brie was surprised by the shooting pain and screamed. She bit her lip afterwards, stilling her thoughts. She had experienced this once before. She knew how to transfer the pain into something sensual if she centered herself.

Brie could hear the concern in Sir's voice when he

got into position behind her, and asked, "Color, téa?"

Although her skin was on fire, she knew she could handle another stroke and she *needed* to take it from Sir. "Yellowish-green, Master."

Master Anderson cautioned Sir, "Concentrate and deliver. Do not hesitate or you will either damage the skin or deliver an inadequate stroke and be forced to do it again."

Brie closed her eyes and smiled to herself. Her Master and she were one in this moment. This would be a challenging test for them both.

Her pussy tingled at the sound of the whip just before it came in contact and transformed into burning fire across her back. Brie did not hold back and screamed in both passion and pain.

Then she felt Sir beside her, his hand running lightly over the mark he had just left on her back. "It looks good on you, téa." He growled into her ear as his fingers traveled up her arm and began releasing her from the cuffs, "You did well, little goddess."

He picked her up and carried her to a chair in the corner. While she rested there, he removed his pants and underwear, revealing his hard cock. Sir lifted her up and sat down, turning her to face the crowd before impaling her on his waiting cock.

Brie moaned loudly, her body grateful to have the burning sensations on her back transferred to fire in her nether regions. Sir pressed her head down and picked up salve from a small table nearby. He rubbed the cool lotion over the marks on her back.

The sensuality of his loving aftercare made her

aroused on an almost spiritual level. Sir grabbed her hips after soothing her back and moved her up and down on his shaft.

She threw her head back as she braced her hands on his thighs to help deepen his thrusts.

Sir's satisfied grunt increased her pleasure. The two moved as one as he powered his manhood into her repeatedly. Time no longer had significance as Brie closed her eyes and gave in to the erotic thrill of Sir's possession.

"Are you going to come for your Master?"

She nodded, readying herself for his command.

"Three... Two..." Brie whimpered in response to his slow countdown. On cue, her pussy began pulsating with her impending orgasm.

"One..."

He forced his cock deep within her and held her still.

Brie's vaginal muscles squeezed and released his cock with their vice-like grip. He answered by grabbing her bound hair and tilting her head back farther as he shuddered deep inside her. Then Sir wrapped his arm around her torso and pulled her to his heaving chest, growling softly, "I love you, téa."

She smiled, lost in the ecstasy of the moment. *I love you, Master—heart and soul.*

Brie stayed in his arms, oblivious to the crowd dispersing until Master Anderson broke into her reverie. "There is another couple waiting for the area, Thane. Would you like me to begin cleaning it?"

Sir released Brie and helped her disengage from him. "No, we will take care of it ourselves."

Brie cleaned the chair and then moved to the 'X' on the floor while Sir dressed and cleaned the cuffs, saving his bullwhip for last. After he finished, Sir commanded Brie to dress, all except her top. Just like her first time with the bullwhip, she was given the privilege of showing off her well-earned marks.

As they moved through the club, Brie found it difficult not to gloat. In one day she had secured the future of her documentary and faced the bullwhip a second time. Her happiness only increased when she saw Mr. Gallant and his wife.

Sir stopped before them and formally greeted the pair. Brie noticed Mr. Gallant had his arm protectively wrapped around his statuesque Amazonian wife, just as he had at the collaring ceremony. Despite his small stature, the man exuded a self-assured confidence that garnered natural respect.

"You both appear to be doing well, Sir Davis."

"We are, Gallant. Fate seems to be smiling down on the two of us today."

"Glad to hear it." He added somberly, "That was quite some unpleasant business with your mother at the Center."

"I do apologize for the unseemly disturbance." Brie noticed that Sir abruptly changed the subject. "Téa, say hello to your former teacher."

Brie's smile was genuine as she addressed him. "It is wonderful to see you again, Mr. Gallant." She loved the man who acted as a father-figure and wise mentor all rolled into one glorious person.

She was pleased when he nodded his approval.

"You're positively radiant, Miss Bennett."

Brie was fairly bursting, desperate to share about her film, but she dutifully kept the news to herself. "Life only seems to get better and better, Mr. Gallant. One of the best things that ever happened to me was stepping into your classroom that first night."

Brie glanced at his exquisite wife and found herself captivated by the brand the dark beauty wore on her upper arm. The lighter color of the raised scar made it very noticeable. The brand itself was a simple pattern of two curvy Ms, one above the other.

She was struck by the woman's serene face and could tell she was devoted to her Master. Yet it surprised Brie that such an elegant woman would allow herself to be branded like that. Brie wanted to ask her about the pain involved, but was afraid Sir would take it as a sign that she was considering it for herself. Instead, she said, "I am curious what your brand symbolizes."

The woman lovingly caressed the raised marks. "Two birds in flight." She smiled at Brie, her foreign accent making her statement that much more enchanting when she answered, "My Master guides me to higher levels of awareness."

Mr. Gallant kissed her shoulder and replied, "In the process, she continues to take me to new heights as well."

Brie put her hand over her heart and cooed, "Aww... that's so sweet!"

Mr. Gallant seemed surprised by her reaction and said succinctly, "Simply the truth, Miss Bennett."

Sir wrapped his arm around Brie's waist. "The natural progression of a healthy D/s relationship."

Brie looked up at Sir in admiration and wonder.

Pinch me now...

Their Disappointment

S ir pressed his lips against her forehead. It was reassuring in nature, but reminded her too much of a benediction—a benediction given just before she willingly walked to her own death.

"How can this go well, Sir?" she whimpered.

"It depends on your definition of 'well', Brie. If you are upfront about the film and answer all of their questions truthfully, then I will consider it to have gone 'well' enough."

His wisdom infused her with confidence. "Yes, Sir. Upfront and honest, that's all I have to keep in mind. The rest of it will fall into place as long as I do not shy away from the truth."

Sir encouraged her further. "Brie, my advice is not to take a negative response as their true response. You cannot know how your parents truly feel until they have had time to adjust to the news. Shock tends to evoke erratic behavior."

"I will try to remember that, Sir."

"In the end, what they desire is the truth, even if it is

difficult to hear."

She took another calming breath and announced with more bravery than she felt, "I'm ready."

He gave her a wink as he exited the car. "As am I..."

Sir opened the door for Brie and together they walked up to the house, a unit—partners in crime.

When Brie's mother opened the door, she greeted them pleasantly enough. "How nice you could make it back so soon after your last visit."

From the living room, her father exclaimed, "There is nothing *nice* about this visit, Marcy. They come bearing bad news, I guarantee it."

Brie shook her head. Why did her father always have to make things harder than they had to be?

Her mom shut the door behind them and gestured the two towards the couch.

Sir stopped and informed Brie, "Before we sit, I was hoping to speak to your father in private."

Brie's eyes widened. *Could it be?* Her heart beat wildly at the thought of Sir asking her father for her hand in marriage.

"Although I do not like this sound of this, I will meet you in the study, Mr. Davis. The ladies shouldn't hear what I have to say. Follow me," her father snarled, rising from his chair.

That left Brie and her mom alone, looking awkwardly at each other.

"Is he asking what I think he is?" her mother asked, sounding stunned.

Brie shrugged, but she couldn't hide her glee. "I don't know, Mom. To be honest, he and I never talked about it."

She sputtered, "Let's hope not... It's too soon... There is no way your father would consent."

As if in agreement, Brie's father yelled loud enough for the neighborhood to hear, "Over my dead body!"

Brie groaned as a heated discussion began. One that was too muffled to understand, although the hostility was easy to hear.

"Why don't we go out on the back porch?" her mother suggested.

"Sure," Brie replied, looking down the hallway in misery. *Poor Sir...*

Once they had settled on the porch swing, her mom blurted, "It sure is hot this summer. We've gotten so little rain—"

Brie couldn't care less about the weather and interrupted her. "Mom, why does Dad have to be so unreasonable?"

Marcy frowned. "I don't think your father is being unreasonable at all, young lady. It has only been a few months since you announced you two were dating."

"But Thane loves me, and he is the most amazing man I've ever met. It is an honor to know him, much less be his girlfriend." *'Girlfriend' sounds so weird...*

"If he loves you, then he won't mind waiting a year or two before making a lifelong commitment. You are only twenty-two. Far too young to consider such things."

"But Mom, weren't you barely twenty when you got married to Dad? You always told me when it's right, it's right, because that's how it happened with you."

Her mother said with an air of superiority, "But we

had known each other for years, darling. We weren't strangers like you two."

"Mom, I would be willing to bet that I know Thane far better than you knew Dad when you two married."

Her mother huffed at her remark. "*We* went to high school together!"

Brie giggled. "Well, Mom, Thane and I went to school together, too."

"What do you mean?"

Brie was too scared to explain it more than once, so she answered, "When Dad and Thane come back out, I'll tell you everything. Just trust me when I say that I am confident in my choice of Thane as my partner, and there are legitimate reasons I feel that way."

They sat in uncomfortable silence as the two men continued to have it out with each other in the study.

Her mother asked, "Brie, do you understand why your father is so protective of you?"

"No, Mom. I'm a grown adult now, yet he still he treats me like a baby."

"Sweetheart, do you remember that incident when you were a child? When you were beaten and stabbed with a needle?"

Brie looked to the floor—for a brief second she felt the stab of the needle, the humiliation and terror of the moment. "Of course I do, Mom. I was scarred by that experience." But then Baron came to mind and Brie physically relaxed. She gazed into her mother's eyes. "Until recently." Brie smiled as she assured her mom, "I'm okay now."

Her mother took Brie's hand in hers and squeezed it.

"I'm grateful you feel that way, but your father has never forgiven himself. It has eaten him inside knowing that he wasn't there to protect his little girl. Since then, your father has done everything in his power to keep you safe."

Brie suddenly made the connection as her entire childhood flashed before her eyes. "Is that why we moved to Nebraska?" she asked in disbelief.

"Of course. He wanted to raise you in a small town, away from gangs and violence. It about killed him to let you move to California after college."

That revelation softened her heart towards her father. All these years he had carried the burden of that terrible day, but she had never known it. Brie tried to ease her mother's mind by explaining, "Mom, I'm an adult now. I don't need Dad's protection anymore."

Her mother squeezed her hand harder. "We love you, Brie. You can't expect us to stop caring just because you're getting older. It doesn't work that way. It's a parent's right to worry."

It hit Brie then just how deeply her news was going to upset her parents. It was so much more than just the embarrassment of the film they were going to struggle with. BDSM seemed like abuse to an outsider. It was imperative she help them understand the truth.

"Mom, you need to trust that I am happy and confident in the life I have chosen. You can see how happy I am, can't you?"

"I'll admit you are glowing today. But just because you are in love now doesn't mean it will last."

Brie smiled, silently asking for patience. "Answer me

this. When you told Grandma and Grandpa you were getting married, how did they take it?"

Her mother rolled her eyes, chuckling when she answered. "They wanted us to wait a few years."

Brie nodded in agreement. "See... I think it is a completely normal reaction for a parent. But it's like you've always said, Mom. When it's right, it's right. I love Thane. We were meant for each other."

"But his age is disconcerting, Brie."

She protested. "It's only eleven years, Mom. When I'm thirty, no one will even bat an eyelid."

"You are twenty-two *now*," her mother stated firmly.

Brie was about to argue the point when both men burst out of the study.

"Marcy! You will not believe what this bastard has been doing to our daughter!"

Brie rushed into the house and over to Sir's side. He sat down on the couch with an air of calm, but she did not miss the flush on his skin. It was nothing compared to her father, who was a deep lobster red.

"Stay away from that bastard, Brianna!"

Brie sat down next to Sir and raised her chin in defiance. "Don't be disrespectful to my boyfriend, Dad."

"Don't you mean 'Master'?"

"Wha—?" her mother gasped.

So Sir did not ask for my hand... Brie realized he'd simply informed her father about his role in her life. It made sense, and she suddenly felt embarrassed for entertaining such a silly idea. She appreciated that Sir was man enough to face her father's wrath head-on, but now it was time to bring her mother into the discussion. With trepidation, Brie began, "Mom, Thane and I have chosen to live a Dominant/submissive lifestyle."

Her mother stared at them in confusion. "What does that mean, Brianna?"

Her father growled, "He acts as her 'Master', Marcy. He chains our little girl up and beats her."

"That's not it at all, Dad!" Brie cried in frustration. She reined in her emotions and turned to her mom, stating more calmly, "Dad is exaggerating. You need to *listen* before you make any judgments about us."

Her father's reply was cold and harsh. "Why would we listen to the girl who is being abused?"

Brie popped off the couch and put her hands on her hips. "Dad, do I look like I am being abused? I love the way Thane makes me feel."

"Brianna," her father snapped, "you know nothing else. You have only had this poor excuse of a man to compare against."

"That's not quite true…" Brie sat back down and took a deep breath before she broke the news. "I have been in the service of several exceptional men."

Her mother's jaw dropped. "Are you a…lady of the evening?"

Brie closed her eyes, biting back the torrent that threatened to escape from her lips. She felt Sir's reassuring hand on her knee and used it to maintain her control.

Sir told Brie, "I have explained to your father the dynamic of our relationship and the fact I was headmaster of the school you were trained at."

"School?" Brie's mother stared at her and then turned on Sir in disgust. "How dare you take advantage of our daughter? You…you *pervert!*" She stood up and demanded shrilly, "Get over here, Brie, right this instant or I'm calling the police."

Brie's nostrils flared as she struggled not to lose it. "We are doing nothing wrong, Mom! It would be stupid to call the police, but go ahead. Be my guest. Make a fool of yourself, see if I care!" Brie faced her father. "I came here to tell you something exciting about my film career. I think you would be proud if you knew, but you refuse to listen so I am not going to tell you. I'll just leave so you can find out about it along with the rest of the world. I don't need to deal with your intolerance."

Her father held out his hand to her. "Brianna, I will listen if you step away from him and tell us your news. I want to know the words you speak come from you and not your puppet master."

Brie was about to refuse when Sir spoke up. "Do as your father asks."

She was surprised by his response, but dutifully got up from the couch and walked over to her parents. Both of them gathered around her in a protective manner. Brie glanced back at Sir. He simply nodded, encouraging her to speak.

She looked at the concerned faces of her mother and father, understanding the time had come to be upfront with them. No matter how this played out, she had Sir's arms to fall into when it was over.

I can endure this…

Brie began by telling them about her documentary and the fact it had been accepted by a popular producer. Her mother sat down partway through her description of the film, looking bereft.

"Brie, you are going to let the world know about your lack of morals?"

"No, Mom. I am going to share the incredible experience I've had and explain in an entertaining way this lifestyle I have chosen."

"So you expect us to be proud of you?" her father said with contempt.

"Can't you at least support me? You can ask me anything. I *want* you to understand why I have chosen submission as my path."

Her mother put her hand to her mouth in horror. "I just realized that everyone in town is going to know what you do. How can I hold my head up ever again?"

Brie was hurt, but needed her mother to be on her side. "Look, Mom, you don't have to agree with what I do, but I would still like you to see the film." She said hopefully, "I brought an extra copy with me."

"I refuse to watch a porno, especially one starring my daughter!" her father fumed. "Brianna, I have never been so disappointed in you in all my life."

"It is not a porno, Dad! You don't know me at all if you think that."

"You're right. I do *not* know you at all. You have become a stranger to me." Her father looked past Brie and added, "Do you understand how much I loathe your 'boyfriend'?"

Brie tried to appeal to his fatherly nature. "Dad, I understand that you want to protect me and I can even appreciate that you think Thane is the wrong person for me, but I'm telling you that I love Sir and trust him completely. I've never been happier or felt more cared for."

She saw a look of pain flit across her dad's face and realized she'd hit a nerve she hadn't meant to. "That man is a bad influence," he stated icily.

She looked back at Sir and smiled. "No. He's the best thing to ever happen to me."

Brie's mom forced a thin smile and said in a curt, parental tone, "I respect you have a will of your own, Brie. You believe this is what you want, but you are too young to know what's good for you. You're easily influenced because of your tender age."

"So basically, in your eyes I am still just a child?" Brie asked incredulously.

"Yes, Brianna," her father affirmed.

"Well then, it all comes back to the fact that I'm legally an adult. I have the right to make this choice. It's my life. I would rather have you hate me than pretend to be someone I am not."

"I could never hate you, Brie," her mother protested, giving her a hug. "But this is not the life I want for you." She tucked a lock of hair behind Brie's ear. "It's morally wrong, sweetheart."

"How? I'm in a committed relationship. What is morally wrong about that?"

Her mother shook her head, not accepting Brie's answer but not having a quick comeback to dispute it.

Her father warned Brie, "Nothing you say will ever convince me that what you are doing is acceptable."

"I understand, Dad. But this is my calling. I can't change who I am, even if it disappoints you."

"Then leave. If my opinion doesn't matter, I don't see any point in discussing this further. You're willfully planning to embarrass us in front of the nation. The truth is, you care more about yourself than your own parents. As disappointed as I am, I *accept* that. But I do not respect your choice of 'partner' or the lifestyle you have chosen."

Brie looked to her mother and whimpered, "Mom?"

She stared at Brie with a look of misgiving. She looked to her husband before stating, "I agree with your father."

Brie was stunned and stood there frozen, as if in a trance. Were these really her parents? The people who had loved and raised her since birth?

Sir's warm voice filled the room. "Brie, I think you have accomplished what you set out to do here."

His gentle reminder helped her to refocus. If this was all her parents were capable of giving at this point, then she would have to accept it. Hopefully, there would come a time when they would welcome her back with open arms—once the shock dissipated. *But if that day never comes...* She looked at them both sadly, bereft at the thought.

Brie couldn't keep the tears back when she told them, "Okay, I will leave because you asked. But consider this: you always taught me to follow my heart, no matter the cost. That's what I am doing now. I hope someday you will understand and be proud."

She took Sir's arm and started towards the door.

Her father declared behind her, "I will *never* be proud of you for this. Never!"

Lesson: His Belts

S ir opened the car door and helped Brie into the rental. She remained silent, still in shock over her parents' rejection. Just before they pulled away, her mother ran out of the house. "Brie, can I have the film? I want to see it before the rest of the world."

Brie gratefully pulled the disc out of her purse. "Of course. Mom, I *want* you to see it. I'm really proud of this film."

"I can't guarantee that your father will ever watch it, but I will. I need to stay connected, even if I disagree with what you are doing."

Tears of gratitude ran down her cheeks. "That means a lot to me, Mom."

Her mother gave Brie a quick hug through the car window before running back into the house.

Brie turned to Sir. "Thank you for getting me out of there before I cracked."

His smile was forced. "I struggled myself, Brie."

She leaned over and pressed her head against his shoulder. "Are you okay, Sir?"

"Your father is a provocative man. His heart is in the right place, but his methods are...off-putting."

Brie snorted with anger. "Off-putting? That's far too kind. He was horrible."

Sir turned towards her. "All I have to do is put myself in his shoes, and it makes it easier to accept his reaction."

"So you told him about us, Sir?"

"I felt it was important to do it man-to-man."

"I'm sorry it didn't go better with my parents."

He started the car and muttered under his breath, "It went...well enough."

Brie sat back in her seat and stared at her parents' home through the rearview mirror as they drove away. Would she ever be welcomed back into her childhood home after this? Even if she was allowed to visit, would she ever *feel* welcomed again?

"We have to give them time," Sir stated with confidence.

Brie sighed miserably. "Yes, they just need time..."

Although Brie was glad to be traveling with Sir again, the pain of her parents' rejection tempered her excitement when he informed her that he was taking her to Italy. She sat down dutifully beside him at the airport gate with a forced smile, trying to hide her feelings of despondency.

Sir handed Brie his phone. "Call Rytsar. Let him

know the secret you've been keeping from him. He's been insufferable ever since we left Moscow."

Brie gave a weak smile as she pressed the speed-dial button for Rytsar and waited. It took several rings before he answered. The Dom shocked her by spitting out a string of irate Russian words before she had a chance to speak. Brie looked at Sir in surprise, shrugging her shoulders.

He smirked as he pointed to his watch.

Brie groaned inside, realizing she'd caught Rytsar while he was sleeping. Sir was evil, on so many levels. She said in her brightest voice, "Hi, Rytsar, it's Brie Bennett. How are you?"

He grumbled more Russian profanities.

"I'm sorry to have called you at such a bad hour, but Sir just gave me permission to tell you my secret."

He growled, "Inform your Master that he's a *mudak*." He paused, and then barked, "Go on."

She blushed when she realized Rytsar was serious. She put her hand over the phone and repeated his exact words to Sir.

"Hang up on him," Sir ordered with a grin.

Although she hated doing it, Brie pressed the off button.

The phone immediately rang back. Sir grabbed the phone from Brie, taking his time in answering it. "What was that, Durov?"

Brie could hear a litany of angry utterances coming from the phone. Sir took his rant with a bemused smile. "For your information, Brie just finished talking with her parents and I was under the impression you wanted to be the next in line to know. Sorry I was mistaken. Talk to you later... Oh... What was that? Ah, you do want to speak to Brie after all? I thought you might." He chuckled evilly. "Who's the *Master* now?"

He handed the phone to Brie while Rytsar was still cussing him out.

"Hi, Rytsar, it's Brie again."

Rytsar immediately stopped his tirade and took a deep breath. "Good morning, *radost moya*."

"I have some exciting news to share!"

He laughed. "I've already deduced it."

She was intrigued. "Please tell me."

"You're pregnant. Why else would you wait weeks and tell your parents first?"

"Oh-em-gee! I'm *not* pregnant, Rytsar. I am too young to have a baby! Are you kidding me?"

She heard Sir chuckling softly. She looked at him, pointing to the phone and shaking her head in amusement.

Rytsar sputtered. "I'm sorry... I meant no offense."

Brie stifled her laughter, not wanting to offend the Dom. "It's fine, Rytsar. I forgive you." She was too excited to hold back the news any longer. "If you can believe it, my documentary now has a popular producer behind it!"

"That's impressive, but why all the secrecy, *radost moya*?"

"We were told to keep it quiet until it was official."

"So, no baby Brie in eight months?"

She laughed at the absurdity of it. "No. Sorry to disappoint you."

"And here I was looking forward to being a *dyadya*. Ah, such is life… Congratulations on your documentary nonetheless. I am honored to have bound and fucked such a talented woman."

Brie was instantly reminded of her warrior fantasy that the Russian Dom had so artfully played out for her. She looked at Sir and blushed. "Um…thanks for the congrats."

"I assume I'm mentioned in your film."

"Of course!"

He said in jest, "Then it is guaranteed to be a hit."

She giggled. "Naturally…"

The blaring sound of their flight being announced over the intercom drowned out his reply. Sir gestured for Brie to give him the phone. She handed it back to him, grateful Sir had given her a chance to share the news with a friend who would be glad to hear it.

After Sir hung up, she thanked him and added, "I needed that, Sir."

"It is important for you to experience the positive along with the negative." He picked up their carry-ons and directed her to the gate. "I trust you will find the next ten hours very positive."

She was already excited to be taking another international flight with Sir, but she was speechless when she saw their first-class setting for the trip. Sir's seating area next to the window looked like a small suite. Not only did he have a large-screen TV, but the length of his private area covered four airplane windows. It was like a hotel room in the sky.

"I never knew there were such things…" she said in

awe.

He sat down in the large leather seat and beckoned her to him. "Have you ever heard of the Mile-High Club?"

She giggled as she sat on his lap. "Isn't that where people have sex in airplane bathrooms?"

He shook his head with an amused smile. "Only if the person is desperate and enjoys unsanitary conditions."

"To be honest, Sir, I never thought having sex over a toilet was very sexy."

"Nor I, although I must say you did a fine job of making it look tantalizing during Master Coen's challenge."

Brie grinned as she recalled her bathroom stall antics involving a camera, clothespins and a naughty hairbrush.

Sir whispered in her ear. "We are about to have sex in the air, little sub. I assure you it will not be on a toilet or in the way you are expecting."

He had her full attention now.

"I don't suppose you will let me in on your wicked secret, Sir?"

He surprised Brie by giving her an answer. "It shall be a lesson on belts."

Being spanked was something Brie found sexually arousing. The idea of being hit with a belt terrified her on a level she could not explain. "Sir?"

He smiled with an ease that reduced her building apprehension. "Tonight you will learn the power and allure of your Master's belts." He produced six leather belts, of varying widths and shades of brown, from his carry-on bag. She suddenly understood why the airport staff had kept Sir behind to question him about his luggage. What man needs six belts on a flight?

"Hold out your hands."

He laid the belts in her open palms so she could feel and smell his tools of choice for their upcoming scene. Brie stared at them with a sense of pleasurable dread. Surely he would not beat her with the six different belts...

She glanced at Sir. His playful smirk, along with his raised eyebrow, begged the question—did she trust him?

A perky stewardess appeared, asking Sir what he wanted to drink. He ordered for them both. "We would like your finest merlot."

"Yes, sir!" the young woman answered cheerily.

Brie pouted as she walked away. "I hate when other women call you sir."

Her Master chuckled under his breath. "I can appreciate that. It's something I do not experience, as téa is not a common word."

"In some ways, Masters have it easier..." Brie teased.

He looked at her with feigned sympathy. "A Dominant is expected to be in charge. That takes much forethought and planning, little sub. Both sides of the coin have their benefits and disadvantages. Thankfully for us, it is a pleasant balance."

Brie wrapped her arms around his neck and purred, "Yes, it is, Sir. Very pleasant, although I am hesitant about your plans on this flight."

He snuck a hand down between her legs discreetly, caressing her femininity. "As I suspected, your hesitancy is also marked by juicy anticipation."

Brie closed her eyes in frustration. Why did her body have to betray her like that? She was genuinely scared, but there her pussy was announcing she wanted what she feared. Being true to her heart, she opened her eyes and faced him. "Sir, belts scare me."

He caressed her cheek with the back of his hand. "But you trust your Master."

She nestled herself against his chest and murmured, "Always."

"Good, because I have been looking forward to this lesson for a long, long time."

Brie muffled her whimper in his shirt. *Will it hurt too terribly much?*

"Here you go, sir, our very best!" The stewardess handed the wine to him with a winning smile—the kind of smile that could set a sub's nerves on edge.

The girl looked at Brie, who was still holding the bouquet of belts, and informed her in an overly friendly voice, "You will need to sit in your own seat, ma'am. The plane is readying for takeoff."

'Ma'am' was not a sexy or respectful title compared to 'sir'. Brie resented that it made her sound like an old lady.

Sir took the belts from her and gave Brie a peck on the cheek before releasing her from his lap. She made her way to her own private seating area across the aisle from his. The middle seats did not have the same level of privacy, but they had all the other luxuries.

Brie started pressing buttons and opening compartments to discover all the amenities the plane offered.

The stewardess cleared her throat. Brie looked up and blushed with embarrassment. How unsophisticated could she get? She was handed the glass of wine and told to buckle her seatbelt.

Sir gave her a weary look after the woman left. "You act like such a child sometimes."

She sighed, disappointed in her lack of decorum. Brie stared at her lap and offered her apology. "I'm sorry, Sir."

"Curiosity killed the cat, Brie. Or in your case, it got her ass whipped."

Brie looked up at him in concern. "Please, Sir. I won't play with any more gadgets, I promise."

He shook his head in disbelief. "I was joking, Brie. Do you honestly think I would punish you for your adventurous spirit?"

"It's just that…you are so worldly and refined, Sir, and I am…"

"Bewitchingly curious," he finished for her.

The engines started up, announcing the beginning of their long flight. Brie smiled at him as she sat back in her seat. She buckled herself in, tightening the seatbelt around her waist, and sighed contentedly. Although he challenged her in daunting ways, Sir was good for her— building her up, helping her to be confident and fearless despite her lack of experience. Someday, she would be the sophisticated woman he deserved to have by his side.

As soon as the airplane rose to cruising altitude, Sir stood up and motioned Brie to him. She looked at the six belts lying beside Sir's seat and began shaking in fear. He noticed when he took her wrist to guide her to his chair.

"Brie, this is going to be a positive experience. There is no need to fear me."

She swallowed hard, whispering, "The belts frighten me, Sir. I'm not sure why."

He slid the privacy partition closed, stating, "Then this is a necessary lesson, Brie."

Brie's heart began to race as he ordered, "Take off everything, including your panties, but leave the skirt on."

She undressed and felt her nipples grow hard. Out of fear or exhilaration? She couldn't tell.

Sir adjusted the seat so that it leaned back at a forty-five degree angle. "Kneel on the chair, ankles at the edge, wrists resting against each armrest."

There was a mirror on the back wall. It faced a similar mirror above the TV screen on the opposite side. Not only did it give the small area a sense of more openness, it also allowed her to look at herself and gave her a limited view of Sir.

He picked up the first belt. Brie expected that he would fold it in half to spank her with it. Instead, he knelt down and secured her right ankle to the chair.

Brie looked into the mirror and smiled. *Belts as restraints!*

She glanced down to watch as he belted her ankle into place. These belts were specially modified, with holes created just for this purpose. It made her wet to think of Sir altering the belts as he contemplated how he would use them on her.

He was quick to belt her other ankle and both wrists.

The fifth belt went around her waist. Brie was unsure of its purpose, but the possessive feel of having his belt cinched around her made her loins hot.

He then took off the chain around his neck and undid her collar. It surprised her, because he'd insisted she wear it on the plane, even though they'd had to remove it while going through security. She was curious why he'd been so adamant about it when he was taking it off now.

Sir placed her beloved collar inside a small drawer, along with his key, and picked up the sixth belt. It was wider than the others. Brie bit her lip as he placed the belt around her neck and tightened it. It was loose enough to feel comfortable, but restrictive enough to keep her aware of its presence.

She looked in the mirror and saw Sir's reflection staring back at her. She was covered in Master's belts. It was an erotic feeling, being bound by Sir like this.

"Who are you?"

"Téa."

"Who owns you?"

"You do, Master."

Sir undid his tie and rolled up his sleeves. Keeping eye contact with her, he unbuckled the belt around his waist and slowly pulled it out of the belt loops. Brie let out a tiny gasp, her helplessness and fear somehow accumulating into something deliciously thrilling.

"Not a sound," he commanded as he lifted her skirt.

Brie was surprised he had not given her a gag. In a public place like this, she would have appreciated it. Instead, he was expecting her to remain in complete control. Then it dawned on her that this was similar to the lesson on the balance beam. She'd had to concentrate on remaining still while he teased her with the electricity of the violet wand.

The man was remarkably wise in planning out his scenes.

Sir grabbed the end of the belt around her neck and applied just enough pressure to focus her attention solely on him. With his other hand, he began lightly slapping her ass with his belt. The sound of the hard leather striking her skin was sultry. The feel was similar to a light flogging.

"Do you like, téa?"

She remembered his command to be silent and only nodded slightly. The belt around her throat did not allow for freedom of movement.

Sir continued to warm her buttocks with the belt, hitting with more power, but not bringing the biting pain she had feared. He concentrated on his work, keeping the tension around her throat while carefully placing the strikes of the belt so that they covered every inch of her skin.

Every once in a while he would stop to stare at her in the mirror. The lust radiating from his eyes made Brie weak.

"We're almost done here," he announced. She watched as he pulled back for a more forceful strike. Brie closed her eyes and squelched the cry that erupted in her throat when the belt made contact with her skin. It was challenging, but not overwhelming. Just enough force to bring biting pleasure.

He let the belt fall, the buckle clanking as it hit the

floor. Then he caressed her skin with his free hand, the hint of a smile playing on his lips. "I shall never tire of this ass."

Sir moved into position behind her. She watched him unbutton his pants and ease his cock out of his briefs. He stroked his shaft several times before pressing it against her wet pussy. Sir pulled a little harder on the belt around her neck, forcing her to arch her back as he slipped inside.

"Good girl," he said quietly.

Not crying out during the session with the belt was nothing compared to keeping silent as her Master fucked her. The unique position he had restrained her in gave him a stimulating angle, one that allowed his cock to rub hard against her G-spot with every thrust.

He upped the sensation by grabbing the belt around her waist and using it as extra leverage to pound her deeper. Brie panted hard, wanting to scream—to fill the airplane with the sound of her pleasure.

She kept her eyes on Sir, in total love and lust with the man who possessed her.

As he reached his climax, Sir threw his head back and grunted quietly. Brie closed her eyes and concentrated on the feel of his cock releasing the warmth of his seed deep within her, while the pressure of the belt at her neck reminded Brie of her place—she was totally and completely *his*.

Isabella

S ir's family lived on an island, an hour's journey by
ferry from the main coast. Brie found that fact
completely enchanting, but the city itself turned out to
be captivating in its own right.

Brie couldn't hide her grin as Sir guided her through
the narrow streets of his father's island hometown of
Portoferraio. The old apartments were charming, with
their brightly painted doors and colorful shutters.

Sir explained as they walked, "People mainly take the
bus or walk here. As you can see, cars are impractical."

Brie looked at the narrow streets and nodded in understanding. She squeezed his hand and announced, "I
prefer walking, Sir."

He placed his hand on her back and guided her
through a group of chatty women. One of them looked
at Sir and then took a second glance. He didn't seem to
notice, but the woman whispered to the others and they
all turned to stare at him. Brie wondered if it was possible the group recognized him.

Sir took her up a steep hill where the street had tiny

steps the entire way up. He led her to an attractive apartment with a vivid red door.

He took a deep breath before he knocked. From deep inside the building, Brie heard a woman complaining. After what seemed an exceptionally long time, the door finally opened and a middle-aged woman complained at them in Italian. However, she stopped midsentence when she saw Sir. He smiled at her and put his finger to his lips.

The woman's eyes widened and then she threw her arms around him. Brie stepped back so they could greet each other properly. The woman grabbed his hand and started dragging him inside, shouting up the stairs.

Sir glanced back at Brie. "I told my aunt to keep it a secret. My grandmother does not know it's me." He winked at her. "This should be amusing."

Brie followed closely behind him, anxious to see the look on his grandmother's face after so many years of separation. She saw a little old lady hunched over in a chair facing the balcony. Sir's aunt touched her shoulder and pointed towards him.

The elderly woman turned and time stood still in the small room.

Her face lit up when she recognized her grandson. The tiny woman struggled to stand as she reached out for him. He was by her side in an instant.

His grandmother grabbed Sir's cheeks, pulling his face close to hers.

"*Nonna,*" he said with tenderness, wrapping his arms around her small frame and picking her up off the ground.

Tears of joy ran down the woman's wrinkled cheeks. "*Nipotino…*"

Brie felt tears prick her own eyes as she watched the touching reunion of grandmother and grandson. She reflected on the pain the old woman must have felt at losing her talented son eighteen years ago to suicide, but that was not all she had lost. She'd lost her grandson as well, due to the traumatic circumstances surrounding her son's death. How tragic for them both…

An elderly gentleman slowly made his way down the stairs from the floor above. He looked at Brie in confusion and then turned to stare at Sir.

"Thane!" he shouted, a toothless grin spreading across his sunken face.

Sir held out one hand to him while still holding onto his grandmother. "*Nonno!*"

The old man was all skin and bones, but had a vitality that filled the room. He took Sir's hand and shook it vigorously, laughing with gusto.

Sir's aunt couldn't contain her excitement and impulsively hugged Brie. She understood the woman's joy and returned the hug, glad to be included in the moment.

Sir gestured Brie to him and said something to his grandparents. The old woman let go of Sir briefly and pinched Brie's cheeks with her thin fingers. "*Grazie mille.*" Brie was shocked when his grandmother kissed her right on the lips before letting her go.

The little old woman grabbed back onto Sir, looking as if she would never release her hold again.

The love flooding the room was overwhelming and the joyous look in Sir's eyes was a sight to behold. Brie had never seen him so open and vulnerable, except on a few occasions when he was alone with her. It made her heart sing to see him truly happy.

Although Brie could not understand a word spoken, she quietly found a seat in the corner and enjoyed the role of silent observer to the jubilant reunion of Sir with his grandparents. It was obvious there was a lot of catching up to do, since words rushed out of the mouths of all involved.

But the chatter stopped the moment the door opened from below and a woman's sweet voice laced with an Italian accent called from downstairs. "Is that you, Thane Davis? Is it really you returning from America?" Sir looked in the direction of the voice and had to act quickly as a beautiful brunette threw herself into his arms.

The entire atmosphere in the room changed. The aunt glanced at Brie nervously and then looked to his grandparents, who now only had eyes for the woman in Sir's arms.

Brie noticed the subtle way Sir held the beauty at bay, but there was no mistaking the look of attraction in his eyes. They knew each other—they knew each other well…

"Isabella, what are you doing here?" Sir asked.

"What do you mean? Why wouldn't I be here, Thane? I ran as fast as I could as soon as I got word you were back!" She tiptoed and gave him a peck on the lips before he could stop her.

Sir held her at arm's length. "Bell…"

The brunette smiled at him playfully, not heeding his

subtle warning. "I have waited all these years because I *knew* this day would come."

Sir directed the girl towards Brie. "Isabella, this is Brianna Bennett."

Brie stood up, ready to shake hands with a woman who looked to be the same age as Sir. However, the color drained from the beauty's face as she stared at Brie. Isabella said nothing to her, focusing her attention back on Sir.

"A friend?" she asked hopefully.

"We're a couple, Bell."

The woman shook her head in disbelief and pushed away from him, then ran down the stairs, crying hysterically.

Sir looked at Brie. "I have to go after Isabella. Stay here." He headed down the stairs, jumping down two at a time to catch up.

The room was suddenly silent and uncomfortable. To escape it, Brie headed out to the balcony. There, she inadvertently witnessed the encounter between Isabella and Sir on the streets below.

Sir held her firmly with both hands, even as the woman tried to pull away. He was talking to her, although Brie could not make out what he was saying.

Isabella began hitting his chest in anger but then collapsed into his arms, sobbing violently. Sir held her like a lover as he comforted the brunette.

It hurt Brie to see it and she collapsed, staring at them through the iron bars. Who was that woman?

Sir's grandfather came out to join her and held out his hand to Brie. She was hesitant to take it, but allowed him to help her back to her feet. He pointed to the sea and began talking to her. Even though she didn't understand his words she pretended to, grateful for the distraction. She listened to the strong timbre of his voice, admiring his commanding gaze, and silently wondered if all the men of Sir's lineage were natural Dominants.

When Sir finally returned, he came straight to Brie and put his arm around her. He said something to his grandfather, who frowned but nodded curtly.

Sir spoke to Brie next. "We are leaving so you and I can talk." He led her from the balcony to the stairs, but stopped to give his grandmother a kiss goodbye. The old woman started arguing with him, holding onto his hand in a death grip.

It was heartbreaking to see Sir attempt to gently pry himself from her tight grasp. The terror on his grandmother's face spoke of her fear that she would never see him again, but Sir's grandfather barked a command and she let go.

Sir guided Brie down the stairs to the sound of the old woman's pleading.

As soon Sir shut the door behind them, he leaned against the building, taking a few moments to gather himself before commanding Brie to walk beside him. While they strolled down the street, he explained, "Isabella was my childhood sweetheart. Our families are extremely close, and it was assumed by all that we would marry when we were older."

"I can tell you have a connection," Brie replied lightly, even though it pained her to say it.

"We were very close...once."

Brie wasn't sure she wanted to know, but she forced herself to ask, "What happened, Sir?"

He took his time to answer her, looking troubled when he finally spoke. "After my father died, I wanted nothing to do with love, marriage, or women." He paused and then stated candidly, "I sent Isabella a letter explaining that I never planned to marry."

Those last words cut Brie to the quick. Even though they had never talked of marriage, she had secretly hoped someday he would marry her.

Sir continued, "I explained in the letter that I would not be returning to Italy and broke off all contact with her. It has been that way for eighteen years. I never considered that Isabella might await my return; that she held onto the belief I would come back for her one day. Unfortunately, that unspoken hope compromised her subsequent relationships."

Brie heard the regret in his voice and her heart constricted.

Sir took her hand and held it tightly. "Both families expected the marriage. I do not doubt that even now they hold out hope." He stopped in the middle of the street and turned her to face him, stating solemnly, "I'm sorry, Brie. I do not know if my extended family will be any more receptive to our union than your parents."

"I can handle it, Sir," Brie assured him, grateful that he was stating his intention to fight his family's wishes.

Sir brushed her cheek with his thumb and smiled before they continued down the street. After several minutes, he let out a deep sigh. "Oh, Isabella… What a waste."

There was nothing she could say in response. It was romantic and heartbreaking that his childhood sweetheart had waited for him all these years. There was a part of Brie that wanted to hate her, but in all honesty, she only had empathy for the woman.

Condor Love

After a day of exploring the island of Isola d'Elba with its luscious greenery, rocky cliffs and mixture of sandy and pebbly beaches, the two were invited to dinner at Isabella's family home. Although Brie wanted to avoid her like the plague, Sir insisted they attend.

"This is my family, Brie. To turn down this invitation would be the same as turning down your parents. We will use this as an opportunity for everyone to meet you. To see the extraordinary woman I see."

Despite the doubts that assailed her, she knew showing a lack of confidence would only cause others to question Sir's choice. It was with a courageous heart she faced the evening with Isabella, determined to act secure in her role as Sir's partner.

Isabella's parents lived in an expensive home on the beach. This was no traditional Italian apartment. This was a modern home with a breathtaking view of the sea. It appeared that Isabella had very wealthy relatives.

Brie was surprised that everyone welcomed her with smiles and hugs. If she hadn't suspected their true feelings, she would have missed the slight reservation in their welcoming embraces.

Isabella came out of the kitchen with a beautiful smile framed by rosy cheeks. Brie was struck by how stunning she was with her sparkling eyes, those perfectly shaped lips and that womanly sway to her hips. "Welcome to our home! I have spent the entire day cooking your favorites, Thane. I had a suspicion you have not had traditional food in a *very* long time." She turned to Brie. "It is my hope that you will enjoy it as well, Miss Bennett. We believe food is an expression of the soul."

Brie understood her meaning. In her own experience, she'd felt closer to Sir whenever he'd shared one of his favorite dishes with her. Because of that, it seemed almost sinful to have Isabella cook for him now. Her jealousy got the best of her and Brie secretly prayed the dinner would be a disaster. Unfortunately, the smells floating from the kitchen belied that hope.

Isabella disappeared again to finish the meal, while the huge family gathered around a massive table and the wine began to flow. Brie watched Sir covertly, noticing how comfortable he was, how frequently he smiled and how easily he laughed. It was heartwarming to see.

When Isabella finally returned, a troupe of women got up to help her, filling the table with a bounty of authentic Tuscan cuisine. Brie quickly glanced over the table, hoping to see tomatoes somewhere in one of the many dishes. Naturally, Isabella knew him too well for that.

Isabella loaded a plate and placed it in front of Sir with a proud smile and a hint of a blush. She then made a similar plate for Brie.

Sir explained to Brie, "You are expected to eat every bite. If you do not, the family will consider it an insult."

Brie stared at the plate piled high with food. There was no way she could finish it all. It felt as if she was being set up for failure with a capital F.

She heard Sir's quiet chuckle. He bit the bullet for her, asking Isabella for a '*piastra*'. Isabella looked at him oddly, but handed him a fresh plate. Sir took a little of everything from the bountiful meal. He slid his plate over to his grandfather, slid Brie's plate in front of him and placed the new one beside Brie.

A hush fell over the table. Sir grinned and rubbed his stomach. "*Non Italiano.*"

The group laughed and began partaking of Isabella's incredible feast. Sir winked at Brie and held up his fork, inviting her to eat.

Although what was sitting on her plate was far more than Brie would eat normally, it was manageable. "Thank you…Thane," she said quietly as she picked up her fork and chose the same item he did.

When Brie tasted Isabella's gnocchi, she closed her eyes and stifled her moan of pleasure. It was soft and light, almost melting in her mouth as she chewed. Her heart sank. There was no doubt that Isabella was a damn fine cook. Why did the woman have to be beautiful, loyal *and* talented in the kitchen?

It was with joy and sadness Brie finished the entire plate. Everything on it, even the seafood items—which she normally didn't like—was simply prepared and delicious. To Brie, each bite had been an added nail in the coffin of her own inadequacy.

After much laughter and lively discussions in their enchanting native tongue, the group retired to a large room with plenty of seating and an expansive window overlooking the coast.

Sir directed Brie to a seat while Isabella separated herself from the family. When Isabella picked up a guitar, Brie's heart sank.

Not this too…

Isabella took a few minutes tuning the guitar and then took a seat on a stool directly facing Sir. She smiled shyly and announced, "I haven't played for years now, but *Papà* insisted. I apologize in advance."

Sir nodded, a silent encouragement Brie recognized. Her seeds of jealousy began to sprout into life. Sitting there next to Sir, Brie felt like she'd already lost him.

Isabella's fingers danced over the strings, filling the room with a soulful melody. Although there were a few little mistakes, they did not detract from the beauty of her song.

Then Isabella sang.

Her voice was disarming, reminding Brie of the tale about sirens who lured seamen to their deaths with their beautiful voices. Although Brie could not understand the words, the emotion behind them was clear. Isabella was singing a love song to Sir.

First with the food, and now with the music, Isabella was making love to Sir through untraditional means. She was reminding him, as well as showing Brie, why Sir had fallen in love with her all those years ago.

It wasn't just Sir Isabella was ensnaring with her

many talents. Brie was equally captivated by the beautiful and talented woman. She knew if she were a man, she would want this woman for her own. A lone tear ran down Brie's cheek at the revelation.

"Are you okay?" Sir whispered.

She wiped the tear away. "The song… It's just so beautiful, Sir."

He looked at Isabella and smiled. "Yes. Yes, it is."

In that moment, Brie's fate was sealed.

She knew what she needed to do, but lost her courage that night. Instead, she lay beside Sir, savoring the warmth of his love for just a little longer.

It wasn't until the next morning that she found the strength, sitting in the little espresso café Sir had taken her to. Brie took a deep breath, praying she would not cry until it was over.

"What's wrong, Brie?"

"Sir… Thane…"

He looked at her with concern. "This must be serious."

She nodded.

"You have my attention."

She looked away from him, unable to keep her composure while looking into his eyes. She stared out of the window at a couple walking hand in hand. That wasn't helping, so she averted her eyes and focused on a bird pecking at crumbs. "You seem happy here, Sir."

"I am," he answered cautiously.

"I have never seen you this way before. It's…wonderful."

"If that is true, why can't you look at me?"

Brie's bottom lip trembled when she spoke. "You belong here, Sir. This is your home. These are your people. You deserve the love and support you've found here."

He shook his head in irritation. "You are not making yourself clear, Brie. Spit it out."

She braved a look into his magnetic eyes and the tears began to fall. "You told me that condors mate for life. I believe that. However, I think there is one instance that can split a pair apart, besides death." She let out a sob and had to stop for a second, swallowing hard to get rid of the lump that had formed in her throat. "I think a condor's love is so strong she will let her mate go if she knows he will be happier with another."

Sir stared at her and said nothing.

Brie closed her eyes and commanded herself to stop crying. She was sacrificing her heart, but she didn't want to do it with tears. His silence let her know she had read the situation correctly.

"Brie."

She opened her eyes, prepared to have her heart shattered for him.

He pushed his chair back and commanded, "Come here."

She did so unwillingly, terrified he was going to have her bow before him to release her from her collar. To her relief, he directed her to his lap instead. She climbed onto it and laid her head against his chest, listening to his heartbeat. It was for that heart she was sacrificing herself.

"I did not understand until this moment how much I needed you to say that."

Her heart broke into a million pieces. Brie held him closer, not wanting to let him go despite her decision to set him free.

Sir nestled his face in her long hair. "I would never have expected such a gift from you."

She answered sadly, "I love you, Thane."

His laughter was low and warm. "Yes, you do."

"Your happiness is everything to me."

"As you are a submissive, I am not surprised you feel that way." He cupped her chin and gazed into her eyes. "But I will never let you go."

"Sir?" Her heart hadn't dared to hope.

"You are mine. There is no other."

"Isabella?"

"Is a part of my past."

"But, Sir, the woman is beautiful, talented and can even cook."

"You are beautiful, talented, and you…are learning to cook," he added with a kiss on her forehead.

Brie whispered, "But Sir, Isabella is an extraordinary woman."

"I concur. However, she and I together do not equal *us*. I am not the boy she once knew. She cannot meet the needs I have now." Sir cradled her cheek in his hand. "You are my soul's complement. I love *you*."

Brie started crying without any chance of controlling

it.

"Would you give up on us so easily, Brie?"

She struggled to answer him through her tears. "No, Sir. I love you too much."

Sir kissed her salty tears. "I believe this is the greatest gift I've ever been given—my happiness in exchange for your heart." He lifted her chin and kissed her gently on the lips. "Silly girl, my happiness is you."

Brie melted into his embrace, the relief of not losing him announcing itself as a painful sob. She buried her face in his chest.

"I am honored by the depth of your love, babygirl." He put both arms around her and held her tightly.

Brie felt an incredible rush, as if she had been reborn and given new life.

Captive

"There is a special place I want to take you, Brie," Sir informed her as they walked down to the docks. He helped her onto a simple sailboat and introduced her to a man she'd met at Isabella's dinner party a few nights before.

Sir explained, "Pietro was a friend of my father's. We used to go sailing together when I was a child."

The older gentleman took her hand and put it to his lips. "*Sei bellissima.*"

Brie blushed, knowing he'd said something about her being beautiful. "*Grazie,*" she replied shyly.

Pietro gave Sir a long and emotional hug. When he pulled away, there were tears in the older man's eyes. It was obvious to Brie that seeing each other brought back treasured memories for both men.

Sir directed Brie to the front of the boat while they set about getting it ready to sail. She basked in the warmth of the sunshine, feeling like the Queen of Sheba when the boat began to pull away from the dock.

Brie secretly pretended this was her boat and they

were her two manly servants. It was a naughty fantasy, considering her place, but she threw her head back and drank in the power and delight the image brought.

Eventually, Sir joined her. He looked incredibly sexy with the wind whipping through his dark hair, like he was meant to be on the ocean as a captain—or a pirate.

He took in a deep breath of the sea air. "I love getting out on the water."

"I do too, Sir. I love the smell and the feeling of freedom it inspires." She looked out over the expanse of blue. "It spurs the adventurer in me."

He pulled her up to stand beside him, holding her close. "It appeals to a part of my soul that lies dormant until I'm on the water again."

She enjoyed the wind playing with her hair. It was a moment she wished she could capture and bottle, to be savored often in the years ahead.

"You see that little island?" he asked, pointing over her shoulder at a speck on the horizon. "That is our destination. My father used to take me there as a boy."

She snuck her hand around his waist and snuggled against Sir, grateful that he was including her in retracing a part of his past.

"It's been more than eighteen years since I've been," he said pensively, as if he was shocked by the passage of time.

Sir told Brie to undress down to her bathing suit while he helped Pietro lower the sails as they approached the tiny island. Brie heard a satisfying splash when the sailor dropped the anchor over the edge of the boat.

The two men talked for several minutes before Sir

rejoined her. "He'll come back in four hours. That should leave us plenty of time to play."

Play? Maybe this was more than a walk down memory lane.

Without any warning, Sir picked her up and threw her into the water. Brie yelped as she fell and the cold sea enveloped her. She popped her head back up and took in a deep breath, only to hear Sir say, "You better start swimming towards the shore, princess. I am about to capture you."

He started peeling off his shirt, looking at her lustfully.

The thrill of the chase infused her with giddy determination. Brie started swimming for all she was worth, heading towards a small alcove on the island. Even though she was smaller than Sir, she was a good swimmer and thought she could make it before he caught up.

She heard a splash. Sir was coming for her...

Brie kept her eye on her destination. He would not apprehend her easily if she could help it. Brie tried not to think about his long, powerful strokes as she swam until she felt hands grabbing at her legs. She screamed and was rewarded with a mouthful of salt water.

Survival mode kicked in as she made her way to the shore, crawling onto the sandy beach gasping desperately for breath. She glanced behind her and saw that he was rising out of the water.

This time Brie let out a terrified scream and jumped to her feet, sprinting across the tiny beach towards a wall of rock ten feet high. She looked behind her and felt butterflies. Sir had the look of a hungry predator about to devour his lunch.

Brie found she was trapped and darted to the right, but he cut off her escape. She switched to the left, but immediately changed direction, trying to trick him. Sir was not fooled, and he lunged.

She sprinted, but he grabbed her around the waist and brought her crashing to the ground. Brie struggled under his weight, fully caught up in the terror and excitement of being captured.

Sir grasped her wrists and pushed them into the sand as he lay on top of her. His low laughter helped to calm her wild struggles.

He ignored her protests as he pulled the strings on her bikini, leaving her naked and exposed. Brie thought he would take her then, but he stood up and threw her over his shoulder, leaving her little suit discarded on the beach.

As he walked towards the rocks, he slapped her ass hard. "Did you really think you could escape me, princess? I could have captured you at any point."

It appeared he was giving her the opportunity to play out a version of her Queen of Sheba fantasy. She tested it out by replying snottily, "Do not touch me, you filthy swine. My father will have your head for this!"

He laughed loudly. "I don't care who your daddy is, princess. Your cunt is mine."

She smiled to herself, thrilled by his choice of scene.

Brie was about to protest when he put her down next to the cliff. "Climb," he ordered, pointing to the rock.

Brie looked closely and noticed someone had carved

handholds into the cliff face. She stepped back and folded her arms across her bare chest. "I will not!"

Quick as lightning, Sir had her bent over and was slapping her ass with enough force to bring tears. She totally deserved it and loved playing the bratty princess. Being a naughty submissive did have its benefits.

When he let her up, she wiped away the tears defiantly, refusing to speak.

"Climb," he commanded.

With her head held high, she faced the rocks and started her ascent, knowing that he was admiring her pinkened ass from below.

When she reached the top, the ground leveled off to a grassy area surrounded by trees and vegetation. It was so beautiful that Brie stopped for a moment to admire it.

She heard Sir moving below her and got her mind back in the game, trying to scramble away as soon as she crested the top, but Sir wrapped his hand around her ankle and pulled her back down to the ground.

He was on top of her in a second, squeezing the breath out of her with his weight. "You must have mistaken me for one of your imperial fools...but I am no fool, princess." He bit her shoulder, causing her to cry out in passion. "You like that, don't you? I bet I know what else you like," he said hungrily, feeling the wetness between her legs. He added, "But I don't care what you want."

Sir pulled her onto her feet and slung her back over his shoulder, carrying her to a dead tree in the middle of the field. He put her down and pressed his large hand against her chest, pushing her against the bark. "Don't move."

"No one tells me what to do," she protested.

He stared into her eyes with such a look of possession it stole her breath away. "I do."

She lost herself in his gaze and nodded automatically.

He smirked. "That's right, princess. I control you." He whipped out a piece of rope from his swim trunks and tied her wrists together before lifting her arms above her head and slipping her bound wrists over the end of a broken branch.

Sir stood back and admired her stretched form.

"Don't look at me," Brie snapped.

"Not only will I look at you," he stated. "I will touch you." He brushed her nipples and slipped his hand between her legs, forcing a finger into her pussy. She gasped, pressing against the tree as she tried not to give into her lust for him.

"I feel your excitement. Your cunt tells no lies." He pulled his finger out and ran her wetness across Brie's lips. "Taste."

She licked her lips and sampled her salty sweetness before turning her head away as if in disgust.

He grabbed her chin and licked her lips. "Luscious…"

Sir thrust his tongue deep into her mouth, plundering her like the pirate he was pretending to be. Brie's body betrayed her, eagerly responding to his aggressive nature. It knew him too well to deny her Master pleasure.

"You are a wanton creature," he teased, leaving her desperate and needy as he looked around as if searching for something. Once he spotted what he was looking for, he left her, stating, "Your captor has better things to do."

Sir walked off leaving Brie bound to the tree. She sighed in contented frustration. She *loved* the way Sir played with her.

Brie watched curiously as he walked up to a crooked olive tree that split into two rickety fingers. He picked up something in the crook of the base and studied it. Then he counted out his steps as he walked farther away from her.

When Sir finally stopped, he rolled a large rock over in a sandy gullet. He knelt on the sand and began digging with his hands.

Brie shook her head, wondering what the heck he was up to. After many minutes of laborious work, she heard him cry out in triumph. She was dying to know what he'd found.

Thankfully, Sir satisfied her curiosity by walking back to her, hoisting a small chest over his shoulder and wearing a charming grin. It gave him a delightfully boyish appearance.

He put down the old chest and unlatched the rusty closure. Before opening the lid, he looked up at Brie and explained, "My father and I came out here to fish and play pirates every summer when I was a boy. He always hid something in the chest for me to find. I didn't think there would be anything this time, but old habits die hard. I had to check, but I can't imagine what he put in here."

Brie watched in fascination as he lifted the lid.

"Ah." Sir pulled out a bottle covered in sand. He

wiped off the label and then sat down on the grass, shaking his head. "*Papà...*"

Brie watched silently from the tree, wishing she was free to go to him.

Sir held the bottle and stared at it as if he was being bombarded with memories. Finally, he spoke. "It is tradition in my family to share a bottle of Brunello di Montalcino as a rite of passage when a boy became a man. My father must have buried it when he visited my grandparents after his last European tour..." He added quietly, "How could he know he would never return?"

"Oh, Sir..." she said sorrowfully.

"No, Brie. I will not mourn him on this island." He looked into the trunk and took out a corkscrew. "I can think of an appropriate use for this wine." He stared at her as he licked his lips. "And I think he would approve."

Sir uncorked the old bottle with a satisfying pop and took a long sniff, closing his eyes to take in the bouquet. "Amazingly, it is still sweet." He lifted the bottle up and nodded at the sky before taking a swig. "Ahh...that's fine wine, *Papà.*"

Sir walked over to Brie and shared the drink with her by taking another long draught from the bottle before kissing her. Red wine flooded her mouth with hints of musky berries and vanilla. She smiled when he pulled away. "That's delicious, Sir."

He cupped her breast and raised his eyebrow. "This is how I plan to enjoy his gift." Sir poured the red liquid onto her breast and leaned in, sucking on her nipple seductively. He lifted her wrists from the branch and untied her before forcing her down on her knees. Sir slipped out of his trunks and poured the wine over his rigid cock. "Suck me," he ordered.

Brie smiled, grateful for the chance to please her Master. As much as she'd enjoyed playing the spoiled princess, her joy was in pleasuring him. She ran her tongue over the length of his cock before concentrating on the smooth head of his shaft. When she pulled away, he poured more wine over it. She opened her mouth and took in the stream of the fermented grapes. It was so wickedly hot to drink from his cock.

The wine ran down her chin and dripped onto her breast. He knelt down and put the bottle on the ground, ordering, "Lie on your back, but lift your ass off the ground."

She lay in the grass and lifted her butt up, spreading her legs for him. Sir ran his hands over her thighs, looking at her greedily. He took a swipe of her swollen clit with his tongue before picking up the bottle and pouring the wine over her pussy. He lapped it up with obvious pleasure.

"The best way to drink wine, babygirl." Sir did it again, drenching her sex with the red wine, but this time he settled in for a long session of cunnilingus. Brie moaned as he took her clit between his teeth and sucked hard before fluttering his tongue over it. She bucked against him, surprised by the intensity. He held her still, his fingers digging into her skin helping to state his authority over her.

She cried out when her pussy began pulsing in pleasure. He did not let up, demanding her climax with his tongue. "May I?" she asked between gasps.

He said nothing, but increased the pressure and tempo of his tongue as he inserted two fingers into her and began pumping vigorously. There was no stopping such aggressive stimulation and Brie's pussy burst with love for Sir.

He lapped up the mixture of wine and her watery juices, groaning in satisfaction as Brie's thighs trembled with aftershocks. He looked up from her mound and growled, "I'm coming for you, princess." He crawled up between her legs to position himself.

Sir took her face in his hands, looking her in the eyes as he plunged his cock into her fiery depths. "There is no escaping me…"

Brie focused on his mesmerizing gaze as he took her as his submissive, his goddess, his lover.

It was difficult to leave Isola d'Elba the following day. The hardest part by far was Sir's goodbye to his grandmother. The tiny woman started crying before Sir even announced they were leaving. She refused to let Sir go, whimpering, "*Non andare via*," over and over again.

Even his grandfather's stern command could not get her to release her desperate grasp on Sir. Brie could not bear to watch him pulling away from the sweet old woman again, and looked away.

It must have broken Sir's heart as well, for he called out Brie's name. When she met his gaze, he asked,

"Would you be willing to return in six months?"

Brie nodded vigorously, thrilled at Sir's suggestion.

He turned back to his grandmother. "*Sei mesi, Nonna.*" She shook her head as if she didn't believe him. Sir touched his forehead to hers and said firmly, "*Sei mesi.*"

"*Promettere?*" the tiny woman whispered.

Sir smiled. "*Sì, Nonna.*"

Her tight grip slowly loosened, but the tears did not stop. She looked at Brie and commanded, "*Promettere.*"

Sir told Brie, "She is asking you to promise that I'll be back."

Brie took the old woman's arthritic hands in hers and said with confidence, "*Promettere.*" Whatever it took, Brie would make certain her grandson returned to her in six months' time.

With a gentle smile on her lips, his grandmother patted Brie's cheek and said in broken English, "Good girl."

Sir took Brie's hand and escorted her down the stairs before the old woman's tears began again. He guided her through the narrow streets, just as he had the first day they'd come to the island, but everything felt different now.

Brie had faced a lover from his past and their relationship had grown from the challenge of it—they were more united as a couple.

She felt the refreshing tonic of the island, the love of his *famiglia,* and the healing power of his father's gift would give them the strength they'd need for whatever lay ahead...

Birthday Girl

Brie woke up wondering if Sir knew.

"Good morning, babygirl."

He grinned as he pulled the sheet away and presented her with a morning gift. Brie took his hardening shaft in her small hand and began caressing it with self-indulgence. Waking up this way was always a treat—making that connection with Sir before the day had a chance to break in.

She swirled her tongue around the ridge of his cock and sighed contentedly as she took the warm head of it into her mouth.

Sir tilted his head back and groaned, making Brie wet with his pleasure. She tasted his pre-come, which signaled that her mouth was exactly what his manhood desired.

"I want you to swallow, téa," he commanded.

She smiled with his cock still in her mouth. Her lips made a popping sound when she opened them to answer. "My pleasure, Master."

She tickled the frenulum with light flutterings of her

tongue before taking the length of him deep in her throat. He grabbed the back of her head and began guiding her up and down his shaft, but it seemed this morning he wanted to take it slow—real slow.

That pleased Brie. When she concentrated on him like this, it invited a spiritual connection with him. As odd as it seemed, it stopped being about getting Sir to climax and became more about pleasing him. Sessions like this could last an hour, and in that time she would read his changing needs and fulfill them, all without bringing him over the edge.

It was during those long morning sessions that Sir would speak to her openly about her triumphs and failures. Always in a positive way that empowered her to succeed in the future.

"I noticed you were more relaxed last night, little sub. I do not think I have ever taken you so deeply in that position before."

Brie looked up at him and smiled without losing her rhythm or suction.

"Your body seems to be much more capable of yielding than it did the first time I taught you that position."

She nodded in agreement, still pleasuring his cock as she listened to his critique.

"Yet I know, téa, as deep as I can force myself into your pussy, there are areas here," he touched her temple lightly, "that you still have locked away."

She opened her mouth to protest, but he pushed her back down on his cock.

"Yes, little sub. I see it in your eyes, that hope I will

not ask this or that of you. However, it is my intent to continue to push. Do not mistake my inaction at this point as future protocol."

Brie's heart rate sped up, wondering what he had planned for her. That welcomed excitement of being his and knowing whatever he asked would open a whole new world of sensations made her tremble inside.

"I, too, have areas I have been hesitant to tread. Just as I challenge you, I test my own boundaries."

He lifted his hand from the back of her head, allowing her to disengage from his cock.

"I love being yours," she purred.

He smiled as he brought her lips back down on his shaft and pushed for deeper penetration down the tight muscles of her throat. She willingly opened and took his entirety.

"That's my good girl. Now play with yourself as I come."

She drank his masculine release as she flicked her clit with enthusiasm. His praise and pleasure were gifts enough on this, her special day.

Sir reached down between her legs and joined in her fingering. Soon her pussy was surging with its own pleasure. He leaned over and whispered, "Happy birthday, babygirl."

That night, Sir presented Brie with a golden corset, a matching thong, black hose and a beautiful pair of stilettos. He told her to put them on and model the outfit for him.

When she came out of the bedroom, he had her turn before him so he could admire her pretty new ensemble from various angles. He whistled in appreciation as he picked up a delicate tiara from the table.

"Come to me, birthday girl."

Brie glided to him and smiled as he placed the delicate piece on her head.

"Perfect," he proclaimed with pride.

His praise was more precious than any gift.

Sir hadn't told her what his plans were for the evening, but the fact she was not wearing anything to cover her shapely bottom let her know it would be an in-house affair.

When the doorbell rang, he said with a mischievous glint in his eye, "Let the festivities begin…"

Sir placed Brie in the hallway and handed her a silver tray. He pulled out a silk blindfold from his suit pocket and told her as he tied it, "Stand still and follow my instructions, birthday girl."

Her body tingled with excitement as she wondered what surprises Sir had in store.

Sir opened the door and stated matter-of-factly, "Set the food in the kitchen, we will serve drinks in the living room."

A stranger's voice answered. "Thank you, Sir Davis. It is our honor to serve you tonight. We will make your night memorable."

"Actually, not garnering my notice would be considered a success by my standards."

"Of course."

Brie heard several people move past her without acknowledging her existence. She quickly surmised they were the caterers by the drifting aroma of exotic foods. After several minutes of listening to them setting up, the doorbell rang again.

Sir answered it and greeted the visitor. "Glad you could make it."

Brie was curious who it was and stood there anxiously, wishing she could take a quick peek.

That was when Sir revealed the game he had planned for the evening.

"As the invitation stated, you are not to speak until you leave your gift on the tray. *But* only give it to téa if she can guess who you are after your kiss."

Brie felt the heat rise to her cheeks as the mysterious visitor walked towards her. However, she noticed there were two sets of footsteps. One was definitely female. It was easy to tell by the sexy click of the woman's heels.

She had to commend Sir. *What a naughty and exciting way for a birthday girl to greet her guests!*

Brie held her breath as the first person leaned over and pressed his lips against hers. The chemistry of the kiss immediately alerted her as to whom it was, but it was the feeling of peace that sealed the deal. Brie smiled while his lips were still on hers.

When he pulled away, she announced confidently, "Tono Nosaka."

"Well done, toriko." She felt him drop something onto her tray. It was so light she surmised it must be a card.

The second person positioned herself for the kiss. Brie was all kinds of nervous, not really wanting to kiss a female. The image of Ms. Clark came to mind and she involuntarily shuddered.

However, her fear was dispelled the instant the soft lips met hers. An unexpected thrill went through her at the intimate contact, despite the gender of her guest. Brie had no idea who it was and silence filled the air as she contemplated who Tono might bring as a date. Thankfully, Brie heard a stifled giggle.

"Lea!"

"Damn, girl, I almost had you stumped and I could have kept my darn present." Lea dutifully placed her card on the tray.

"Do you have a joke for me?" Brie asked half-kiddingly.

"That's your present, girlfriend."

Brie pouted. "Then you can take it back, Lea. Really, I insist."

Lea patted her cheek in a motherly way. "No, sweetie. I'm not rude like you. While you stand there looking all pretty, I believe Tono and I will enjoy the delicious yumminess coming out of the kitchen."

Are Tono and Lea a couple now? Brie wondered.

"Yes, please enjoy," Sir told the two. "Since you are our first guests, they are still setting up the bar, but y—"

The doorbell rang, announcing new mystery guests.

Sir excused himself to answer the door.

Brie quivered. Who would be the next to kiss her? The pressure of guessing was exhilarating, but failure would be humiliating—there would be embarrassment for both parties if she guessed wrong.

Sir gave the same directions and a single male walked over to her. He lifted her chin and kissed her possessively, teasing her with his skilled tongue. Brie knew that kiss, but could not believe it.

"Rytsar?"

He placed his gift on her tray. "*Radost moya*, we meet again…"

Brie heard Sir slap his back with excessive force. "It was supposed to be a simple kiss, not an invasion."

Rytsar chuckled and answered with his seductive Russian accent, "I could not resist."

The two moved off to join Tono and Lea, leaving Brie alone. It was interesting to be the center of the party, but to play the role of blind observer.

She heard the clinking of glasses and Rytsar's guttural laughter just before the doorbell rang again. Brie bit her lip as she felt Sir walk past her to answer the door.

This time it was a large group of people, all laughing and chatting. She distinctly heard Headmaster Coen's voice and felt sure he would be an easy one to pick out.

Most of the group moved past her and went directly to the kitchen. Only a few stayed behind to deliver gifts.

Brie couldn't help smiling when the first leaned over to kiss her. The scent of perfume let her know this was *not* Headmaster Coen. The woman's lips were supple and she surprised Brie by slipping a little tongue across her closed mouth.

Brie pulled back in astonishment. Which woman would dare to kiss her so brazenly? Brie shook her head, knowing the female was the wrong height to be Ms.

Clark. That left only one person in her mind.

"Mary?"

"Seriously? There is no way you could know it was me." Mary pressed her fingers on the edges of Brie's blindfold. "You must be able to see. I thought for sure the tongue would throw you off."

"Ha! It was the fact you were so bold that gave you away, but I'm surprised you came. Last I heard, you'd disowned me."

"I had a little talk with Sir Davis and he persuaded me that you still need me. Who am I to deny such a convincing man, especially when I know he's right?" Mary grabbed Brie's chin and shook her head back and forth forcibly. "And aren't you just the cutest little gift table? Hope you like standing there while the rest of us enjoy your party."

Brie grinned. "I hope your present is worth the lackluster kiss you just gave me."

Mary grabbed her face in both hands and gave her a long and overly passionate kiss that left Brie breathless. Blonde Nemesis leaned in close and said affectionately, "Bitch."

Brie heard the shifting of feet and knew that Mary's little performance had been appreciated by the male population watching.

"I'm off to get a rum and cock. Oh wait, I meant Coke..." Mary's laughter trailed behind her.

The next person took the tray from her before pressing his lips lightly on the back of her hand. The sweet but nonsexual gesture gave his identity away.

Brie bowed her head, pleased that he had come. "Mr.

Gallant."

"Very good, Miss Bennett. Happy birthday. Another year down, a lifetime yet to enjoy." He handed back her tray and placed his gift upon it.

The person who followed wore aftershave, which hinted at his gender, but the kiss was sweet and gentle. When he pulled away, Brie furrowed her brow. Although it seemed remotely familiar, she was stumped. It was comparable to seeing a face she knew but could not place.

Brie tilted her head. "Could you kiss me again?"

Sir answered for him. "No, téa. Only one kiss allowed."

Brie sighed nervously. No one was coming to mind—she had no answer to give. "I'm not sure, Master."

"Still, you must provide a name," he insisted.

The possibility of being wrong in front of all these people was daunting. She stood silently, going over every Dom she'd been with.

Her guest took pity on her and leaned in, rubbing his cheek against hers. When she felt the hard scar tissue, Brie broke out in a smile, thrilled to be in the presence of the Dom.

"Captain."

"Yes, pet. Happy birthday. I must say, you look lovely collared."

She blushed with pleasure, grateful to be reconnected with the military hero. "Thank you, Captain. My birthday has been made better because you are here."

He chuckled lightly. "That is kind of you to say, pet."

He placed his envelope on the tray and moved on.

A large hand with beefy fingers grasped her shoulder and firm lips met hers. There was no doubt who it was.

"Headmaster Coen," Brie said with a coy smile and bow. "I am honored you came."

"Tonight I'm simply Master Coen. No pomp and circumstance allowed."

"Yes, Master Coen."

Brie became curious when the next man stood before her and patted the top of her head as if she were a little girl. She was surprised, realizing that the man did not want to kiss her. Who would Sir invite who would react in such a way besides Mr. Gallant? Well, the answer was simple enough.

Brie grinned as she greeted him. "Mr. Reynolds!"

"Happy birthday, Brie." He placed his card on the tray, adding, "I miss you at the shop, but I hear big things are ahead for you. I couldn't be prouder. Congratulations. It couldn't happen to a nicer person."

"Thank you, Mr. Reynolds. Do you realize if you hadn't given me the job at the tobacco shop, none of this would be happening now?"

He said firmly, "Nonsense, Brie. I guarantee you were destined for success no matter how it found you. It is my pleasure to know such a fine young lady." She blushed at his kind words.

Mr. Reynolds moved to the side to make room for the final guest. She could smell his unique, spicy scent as he leaned forward, which alerted her to his identity even before he kissed her. Baron's thick lips pressed against hers, causing a pleasant warmth in her nether regions.

"I know you…" she murmured during his kiss. When he pulled away, she added, "Thank you for coming, Baron."

He dropped his envelope on the tray. "It's good to see you glowing like a birthday candle on your birthday, kitten."

"I'll never forget what you did for me, Baron. You literally saved me that night at the Kinky Goat."

"And I will forever be in your debt," Sir stated beside her.

"No, Sir Davis," Baron said with conviction. "You introduced me to Adriana. Even though we are parted, I am a better man for having known her. The debt of gratitude is mine."

Brie could hear the thudding sound of Sir patting Baron's muscular shoulder. "We all miss her. She was a remarkable woman."

It wasn't until then Brie understood that Baron had not broken up with his submissive, as she had first assumed. Her heart broke for the kindhearted Dom. "I didn't know she died, Baron," she whispered.

"Do not let it trouble you, kitten. This is your special day. Keep glowing; it makes me happy to see it."

She forced a bright smile, even though her heart hurt for him.

"That's better," Baron complimented.

She heard Sir walk away with him.

The party was in full swing. Brie caught snippets of conversations, much laughter, and the tinkling of glasses and utensils on plates. It was surreal but strangely exciting to be on the outside listening in. Brie cherished

Sir's ability to think outside the box. He had given her an experience she could never have imagined and would never forget.

The Uninvited

This time when the doorbell rang, Sir ran his fingertips over the swell of her breasts as he passed. Brie purred, aroused by her Master's touch.

"Good evening," Sir said when he opened the door. "I was concerned you wouldn't make it tonight. Please come in and kiss the birthday girl."

Brie was glad to hear manly steps, afraid that Ms. Clark might join the party. The new guest stopped before her and waited.

After several moments, Brie licked her lips and giggled nervously. Did he expect her to do something first?

The wave of masculinity that washed over her when their lips finally touched rendered her speechless.

"Well, téa?" Sir asked.

She answered quietly, "Marquis."

"Yes, pearl. Celestia wanted to come tonight, but family obligations took precedence. She hopes you understand."

"Of course, Marquis Gray. Please let her know that she was missed."

He placed their gift on the tray. "I will tell her that." Marquis added as a side-note to Sir, "You should consider strapping her down with her ass bare next year. I am curious if she would be as adept at knowing who canes her."

Brie trembled at the suggestion.

"Sorry, Gray. That privilege is mine and mine alone."

"A pity."

Sir responded sarcastically, "But let me show you to the kitchen. I believe there is an egg dish with your name on it."

"Oh, I wouldn't leave your station just yet, Sir Davis. I saw two guests parking as I entered the building. They should be arriving shortly."

A few seconds later the doorbell rang. Master Anderson's laughter filled Sir's apartment.

This will be easy…

His laughter suddenly stopped as if he had just remembered the rules to the game. Heels clicked up to her first. Brie held her breath as the smell of Cashmere, a perfume she found particularly alluring, enveloped her.

The woman's lips were firm, but inviting and her kiss compellingly feminine. Brie had never thought kissing a woman could be this much of a turn-on, but she found herself aroused by the gentle yet commanding kiss.

When she pulled away, it left Brie confused. Who would Master Anderson bring along with him who could kiss like that?

She would have considered Candy, the sub she had met on the subway, but she immediately dismissed her as a possibility. It had to be someone she knew well. Sir had been consistent in that part of the game.

"I honestly don't know, Master."

"No guesses, téa?"

Brie strained her eyes underneath the blindfold, wishing the material was thinner. She shook her head. "That kiss has left me confused, Master."

Brie could hear chuckles throughout Sir's apartment.

So it was a trick. Was it a man dressed and perfumed as a woman? *No…those lips were definitely feminine.*

"No gift for you," Ms. Clark replied frostily.

A cold chill ran down Brie's spine. *No!*

The mere thought of enjoying her kiss made Brie nauseous. She suddenly understood *exactly* how Ms. Clark had felt when Brie had given the Domme cunnilingus. It was not a pleasant feeling to be aroused by someone you disliked. If she could, Brie would have wiped her mouth to rid herself of the lingering sweetness of that damn kiss.

Master Anderson took pity on Brie and kissed her soundly, erasing the taint of that unwelcomed encounter.

"Thank you, Master Anderson," Brie said with sincere gratefulness.

He placed his gift on the tray. "I forgot we were playing this little game or I would have kept silent at the door."

"Admit it, you're just a loudmouth," Rytsar replied, coming up to join the conversation.

Brie giggled, enjoying the camaraderie of the three Doms who'd attended college together.

Sir moved beside Brie and was in the midst of taking off her blindfold when the doorbell rang again.

"Odd…" Sir muttered as Master Anderson answered the door for him.

The air seemed to leave the room when the door opened. No one spoke a word. The silence was deafening and made Brie exceedingly uncomfortable.

Finally, Brie heard Faelan growl, "What kind of game are you playing, Davis?"

Sir left Brie's side, stating angrily, "Rest assured, you were *not* invited to tonight's celebration."

"I was told to come to this apartment and deliver a note to a man named Alonzo."

"By whom?" Sir asked, his voice deathly calm.

"A woman by the name of Elizabeth. So tell me, *Sir* Davis, who the fuck is she? And who the hell is Alonzo?" Brie could hear the building ire in Faelan's voice.

Neither Dom was someone to trifle with. Brie knew things were about to get ugly between the two as she felt the negative energy crackling in the air. Brie ripped off her blindfold just as Mary moved past on her way to Faelan.

Sir answered Faelan tersely, "Neither are any of your business, Wallace. As far as I'm concerned, you can take that letter and shove it up her ass."

Mary smiled at Faelan as she approached the seething Dom. "It appears this 'Elizabeth' person was playing some kind of joke. Why not have a little fun at her expense? I can think of several things we can do with this letter. Shall we discuss it over dinner? Say, at my place?"

Faelan glared at Sir as if he was still convinced this

had been Sir's doing, but he left without incident. Mary followed closely behind, obviously pleased with herself.

Sir shut the door, but Brie could feel the rage radiating from him. Rytsar grasped his shoulder. "Don't let her win the day."

Sir nodded. He glanced at Brie. It pleased her to see the ire slowly melt away from his countenance as he gazed at her. Finally he said, "I think I must turn you over my knee and spank you, téa. I did not give you permission to take off the blindfold."

Relief flooded her soul as Brie looked to the floor, hiding her smile. "Yes, Master. I need to be punished."

He strode over and took the tray from Brie's hands, handing it to Master Anderson, and informed her, "You will open these another day."

Sir picked her up and slung her over his shoulder, carrying her into the living room. Seeing that the couch was already occupied, Sir laid her over the taller curvature of the Tantra chair so that her ass was in perfect alignment for spanking.

"I think twenty-three swats are in order, don't you?"

The group voiced their approval.

Sir ran his hand over her bare ass cheeks before delivering his first smack. The sound of it echoed through the room and was forceful enough to make her skin tingle pleasantly.

"One..." Sir called out.

Brie looked up to see Lea grinning at her.

Oh, this is fun... she thought.

She let out a squeak at the second, more commanding swat.

"Harder," she heard Rytsar assert.

Sir was not one to follow another man's order. "Two…" He delivered a feather light smack and then followed it up by teasing her clit through the thong.

"Did all that kissing turn you on, téa?" he inquired, before slapping Brie's ass solidly twenty-one more times. Brie loved every minute of it as her friends watched her receive her full set of birthday spanks.

Sir ended it by saying, "Happy…"

Brie whimpered as he called out each word and spanked her with enthusiasm. "…birthday…my…tasty…little…sub."

Her buttocks smarted after his birthday wish. Sir rolled his finger over her pussy, the gold material soaked with her desire. Then he bent down and delivered a tender kiss to her red ass, whispering into her ear, "I plan to play with you tonight, princess. After your little party is over."

That simple comment had her dripping with anticipation.

He helped Brie off the chaise and gestured to the servers. One hurried over and presented two identical martinis to him on a golden tray.

Sir took them both and handed one to Brie. He looked to the friends gathered and said, "I raise my glass to this remarkable young woman beside me, in honor of the day she graced the world with her divine presence."

Brie was both pleased and embarrassed by his words. She gazed at the smiling faces of her friends and trainers, feeling a tremendous sense of joy.

Sir continued. "Here's wishing her much success in

her blossoming film career."

"To Brie's future," Rytsar echoed.

Everyone raised their glasses in unison and drank to the toast.

Brie was overwhelmed and found it difficult to speak. "Thank you for coming tonight…and thank you for helping me grow as a person." She felt she might cry, so Brie finished quickly with, "I have never known such happiness."

The night played out like a beautiful fairytale, except for one uncomfortable moment.

Brie couldn't help noticing Ms. Clark staring at Rytsar the entire evening. There came a point when it became obvious to Brie that the Domme had finally determined she would engage the Russian Dom.

Ms. Clark presented herself before Rytsar and then sank to her knees in supplication. The whole room fell silent.

Sir quickly moved over to her, hissing, "Don't. This is not the time or the place."

Rytsar's icy stare made it apparent that Ms. Clark's dramatic gesture had not been appreciated. *What can Ms. Clark have done to the man to evoke such a callous response?*

The Domme raised her chin haughtily as she stood back up. "Another time, perhaps." She left the party soon after.

For the first time, Brie's heart ached for the woman.

Ms. Clark had just humiliated herself in front of her peers in the hopes of reconciling some past mistake with Rytsar, and been unequivocally shot down.

The Russian Dom, although a sadist, had always seemed a thoughtful and generous man. Brie had to assume whatever Ms. Clark had done to him must have been something truly unforgiveable.

To witness such a scene was uncomfortable for all, but especially hard for Lea. She glanced at Brie. It was obvious how upset Lea was to see Ms. Clark hurting, but she did not leave Tono's side to run and comfort the Domme. That really surprised Brie and made her realize that she needed to arrange private 'girl talk' time with Lea. She was determined to find out what was going on with her best friend.

The tension in the room eased soon after Ms. Clark's departure, once Master Anderson decided to play a humorous round of 'pin the tail on the *pony*' with a willing sub. Brie had never laughed so hard in her life.

But the night turned into something intensely memorable when the server came out carrying her birthday cake. He set it down on the coffee table so everyone could admire it.

Brie walked up and put her hand to her lips when she saw the design. In the middle of the sheet cake were two condors flying around a yin-yang symbol. But it wasn't the traditional black and white design. The light side was represented by the sun and the dark side by the moon. Meaningful to Brie on so many levels...

Sir said tenderly, "Make a wish, Brie."

Her lips trembled as she attempted to blow out the

candles, but it took several tries because she was so touched. She shrugged afterwards, explaining to her friends, "Oh, well, I didn't need a wish anyway. I already have everything I want." She smiled up at Sir.

"That's so cheesy, Brie," Lea teased.

Everyone laughed at Lea's perfect pun.

Brie grinned unashamedly. "Sorry, girlfriend. It's the truth."

She glanced around the room packed with people she held in high esteem, appreciating how incredibly lucky she was. As the festivities began to wind down, Brie found herself staring at Sir from across the room. He was laughing with Rytsar and Marquis. Sir looked genuinely happy—as happy as he had been in Italy.

She realized that he had made a family here that was every bit as dear to him as his blood relatives. This was the life he had purposely chosen.

Sir must have felt her gaze, because he glanced in Brie's direction. Her heart fluttered when he winked at her. How was it possible that one man could captivate her heart and soul?

As she continued to stare at him in loving admiration, a calm resolve flowed over Brie. She knew with clarity what she desired—what she *needed* to make her happiness complete.

Birthday Presents

The moment the door had shut behind the last guest, Sir swept Brie off her feet. He did not speak as he carried her to the bedroom.

Her heart fluttered when she looked into her Master's eyes. There was no doubt he had special plans for his birthday girl. Brie buried her face in his chest and grinned. There was no better gift than to be Sir's plaything.

"Gold suits you, téa, but I prefer nude," he stated as he set her down next to the bed. He turned her around and unhooked the corset, then let it fall to the floor. Sir traced the lines left on her skin made by the corset laces, sending pleasurable sensations to settle between her legs. His fingers deftly relieved Brie of her panties as well.

"Yes, much better," Sir complimented. He pushed her gently onto the bed, grinding his hardening cock against the flesh of her ass.

"What should I try tonight that I haven't tried before?" Sir mused. He disappeared into the closet and returned with golden anal beads, a hairbrush and a delicate ball gag. He held up the metal gag and smiled charmingly as it swung back and forth in his hand. "Only the most beautiful ball gag for my birthday girl."

Although Brie was charmed by the elegance of the gag, the anal beads concerned her. "It's my first time with the beads, Master."

"I'm aware of this, téa. I enjoy introducing you to firsts and this one's been long overdue."

He seemed to be waiting for a response. Brie smiled to reassure him, opening her mouth to accept the gag. Normally, she did not care for ball gags but this one was unusually cute.

The metal ball was smooth and cold against her tongue. Sir secured it in place and turned her back to face him.

"Ah, my beautiful girl..." His hands ran down her curves to rest on her fleshy rump. He leaned over and growled into her ear, "I'm going to fill you with golden beads and slowly draw them out at the peak of your orgasm." Brie gasped as his thumb caressed her anus and he lightly applied pressure. Her pussy pulsated in response to his touch, despite her misgivings.

Sir left her side to turn on the stereo. Brie smiled when she heard the passionate melody of a lone violin. She was sure it was Alonzo's; the intensity of his playing added to the atmosphere in the room.

Sir took the lubricant off the bedside table and began liberally coating the metal beads. Each one was larger than the last, strung together with black cord.

Brie watched him work with curious fascination. It was humorous to think she had enjoyed butt plugs, the insertion of a long, flowing tail and even the challenge of double penetration, but never a common strand of anal beads. She was actually nervous.

Though she was an experienced sub, there were still a few items she found wicked and forbidden, and anal beads happened to be one of them. She assumed it stemmed from a childhood incident when she'd played a game of Truth or Dare with some neighborhood boys...

****

The twins were the same tender young age as Brie, so it didn't seem weird to her when Marcus and Tommy suggested playing Truth or Dare in the backseat of their daddy's car. Cloaked in the darkness of twilight, she didn't feel any shame when they dared her to get naked in front of them. It seemed natural at the age of six. Besides, she'd been equally curious what boys looked like close up.

Everything was innocent enough until one of the boys produced a toy with pretty beads. Marcus said he'd found it in his mommy's dresser, and dared her to stuff the plastic beads up her butt. When she baulked, he assured her that if she did, he would try too. The over-eagerness of the boys frightened her a little, but she wasn't a quitter or a cheater—which was what they were calling her.

Brie took the beads from him, but wasn't really sure what to do. When Marcus offered to help, she agreed and turned around, laying her chin against the top of the seat while she gazed out of the car's rear window with her naked butt in the air.

Just as he pressed the first bead against her tiny hole, head-lights flooded the car. The boys' mother was coming home from work. The woman jumped out of her car and raced to them, screaming hysterically. The boys whined as they desperately tried to dress, begging Brie to get her clothes back on.

****

It had been a bad experience for all three; the lectures, the punishment, the shame…

"Lie down on the bed, téa, legs tucked under so your ass is presented."

Brie climbed onto Sir's bed, closing her eyes and sighing anxiously. Even though she was twenty-three now, and it was Master who wanted to play, there was a part of her that was leery of that simple sex toy.

Sir put the beads down and began rubbing and kneading her buttocks. Brie purred, letting the past melt away.

"That's it, babygirl. No reason to tense."

Brie automatically whimpered when he pressed his finger against her sphincter.

"You will find this enjoyable, téa. Relax…"

She trusted Sir and willed her body to allow his play. Sir swirled the smooth bead around her sensitive anus, teasing her with it before slowly inserting the bead inside. Her muscles stretched and then eagerly clamped around the golden bead, giving her a sense of fullness.

Sir began teasing her with the second one, which was slightly bigger than the first. "One by one, you will take all my beads," he stated, gently forcing them inside.

Brie moaned softly, liking the feel and challenge of the beads as well as the mystery of how they would feel when he pulled them back out. Each insertion felt like a delicious invasion; each tiny surrender made her wet.

"Good girl," he complimented when he was done. Sir stood back to admire his work. "You have the look of a toy, babygirl. All I have to do is pull on the string to bring you to life."

Brie looked behind her and smiled as she swayed her heart-shaped ass seductively as if to say, *Please play with me...*

Sir picked up the brush and Brie readied herself for a swat. Instead, he took a handful of her hair and brushed it. Her scalp tingled from the contact of each individual bristle and she purred. He brushed through her long mane again, tugging lightly on it before running the brush through it.

She lifted her head back, her eyes half-closed in pleasure.

Sir said nothing as he continued to run the brush through her locks, continuing the movement down her back, past the ends of her hair. The bristles grazed her skin, caressing her with tiny points of ecstasy.

"Ooomm..." she moaned with the ball in her mouth. What he was doing felt so sensuous and loving.

Sir brushed her hair slowly and meticulously, stimulating her back with the instrument. Then he stopped and grabbed her waist, thrusting his shaft into her pussy several times before resuming the brushing.

It was delicious, the tantalizing myriad of sensations: the tingling, the light scratches, the fullness of the beads and Sir's commanding cock. She wished it could go on forever; however, Sir had much more in mind for Brie that night.

"On your back, téa, legs wide open."

She lay on the bed, moaning as she watched Sir kneel down and bury his face between her thighs. She arched her back as his tongue lapped her wet pussy just before unleashing its divine torture on her clit.

Panting and moaning soon filled the bedroom when his middle finger found its way inside her, and Sir began caressing her already swollen G-spot. He played her pussy in tune with the song, increasing the sensations to a concentrated level, only to ease away when the tempo changed. He knew his craft well, building her impending orgasm to startling heights.

Brie thrashed her head back and forth, craving blessed release.

Sir looked up from between her legs and chuckled. "Shall I take pity on my birthday girl?"

She nodded vigorously, the metal ball preventing her from screaming, *Please, I beg you!*

"Lay your head back, téa. Close your eyes and concentrate on the sensations I am about to create."

Sir began swirling his finger around her G-spot as he pulled the string attached to the beads taut. Brie's heart skipped a beat in anticipation, but suddenly he stopped. Sir reached up and undid her ball gag. "Eyes closed, my little sub, but I want your mouth open and vocal."

She smiled, remembering her first critique on the very first day of her training. "Yes, Master."

Sir resumed his ministrations, making her loins blaze with desire as he aggressively caressed her pussy. He pulled on the string, causing Brie to momentarily stiffen in fear. *Will it hurt?*

"Relax, babygirl. Let your Master have his way."

She concentrated on the raging orgasm, teetering on the precipice. "Have your way, Master," she pleaded.

A powerful contraction gripped her when his lips met her clit. She had no control now…

When the next contraction hit, Sir began slowly pulling out the first bead. Her body was a hotbed of electrical bursts, but the sensations instantly became focused on the erotic pressure of the bead, causing her anal muscles to spasm with orgasmic energy.

A new sound escaped her lips. It was the cry of her inner animal voicing its satisfaction.

Brie's body took over—her hips thrust upward; her thighs trembled uncontrollably from the intensity and longevity of the orgasm as Sir continued to tease her to climax by slowly and calculatedly pulling out bead after golden bead.

There was nothing left of her when he was done. She was floating on a cloud of sensations, sexually content on a level previously unknown to her.

Brie heard her Master's voice calling to her through the erotic mist in her mind. She had to focus on it to understand what he was saying. "Birthday girl."

Her eyes fluttered open and a slow smile spread across her lips. "Oh, Sir…"

He leaned over and kissed her forehead before collapsing beside her on the bed. "I take it you liked your gift?"

"Best present ever…"

He wrapped his muscular arm around her and let her continue to ride the ecstasy of the experience. Cuddling with Sir was just as prized as the mind-blowing sex.

Eventually he nuzzled her neck. "I was somewhat concerned tonight."

She turned her head and gave him a questioning look. "About what, Sir?"

"What your response would be to the beads."

"Why? I love everything you do to me."

"Your father informed me of your past experience with them."

Her jaw dropped. *Sir knew?*

"I fully expected you to tell me your history with the beads, but you never said a word."

Brie's mind was still reeling at the fact her father had told Sir about that humiliating experience. "But why would my father tell you, Sir?"

"He felt certain that childhood experience damaged you to the point you were susceptible to participating in similarly base activities. I assured him that you had shown no interest in anal beads, which seemed to pacify him somewhat." Sir raised his eyebrow. "Little did he know that he had given me your next lesson."

"I can't believe my father told you," Brie cried, covering her face.

Sir took her hands away and gently laid them on her chest. "I am grateful he was forthright since you failed to be as open."

Brie met his gaze, needing him to understand. "Sir, it's just that I trust you completely. I knew you wouldn't hurt me."

He ran his fingers through his hair. "Communication and trust are the foundations of our relationship, téa. I should never walk into a scene unaware that it holds a possible trigger for you."

"You're right. I'm sorry for putting you in that position." She lowered her eyes, but soon snuck a peek at him, curiosity driving her to ask the obvious question. "What else did my father share with you?"

He smiled, raising his eyebrow mischievously.

Brie stuck out her bottom lip when he did not answer, pleading with her eyes.

Sir chuckled and rolled off the bed to grab her tray of gifts. "Ready to open your presents?" He must have known he had her, because there was no way Brie could pass up a chance to find out what was inside all those envelopes.

He laid the tray on the bed and rejoined her. Brie searched through the gifts, wanting to open Lea's first. She grinned at Sir. "I can't wait to find out what she got me!"

His smirk belied the fact that he already knew.

Brie ripped open the envelope and read her message:

I have created the perfect gift for you, Brie! I can hardly stand having to wait. Turn the card over to reveal your special surprise.

She grinned at Sir as she turned it over, but then her smile disappeared. There was nothing written on the back. It was completely blank.

"Is this a joke?" she asked, waving the card at Sir.

He chuckled. "She's *your* friend."

Brie tossed it on the bed, formulating a plan to get even with the girl. She picked up Tono's envelope next.

"Interesting that you would choose that one," Sir commented off-handedly.

She tilted her head, now curious. "Why?"

"Their gifts are interconnected."

Brie giggled. "So Lea *did* get me a present after all!"

She was much more careful when she opened Tono's. He'd used special rice paper and painted his signature orchid on the front. She pulled out the thin parchment and read a simple haiku, each line written in traditional Japanese script, with the words written in English for her underneath:

Together as one

In desire and spirit

An erotic gift

Brie read it several times, but was unsure of its meaning. "Sir?"

He smiled, but shook his head. "Your surprise is not for me to reveal."

"But you know what it is?" she queried.

"Yes, little sub. There will be no more questions on the subject."

"Are all the gifts going to be equally mysterious?" she pouted.

He held up the tray and winked. "There's only one way to find out."

Brie took Rytsar's from the pile because it was extra thick and promising. What she pulled out looked like an official government document, but it was written in Russian. She held it up for Sir to see. "I don't know what this is."

He took the document and looked it over. A slow grin spread across his face. "It appears that Durov has given you the cabin by the lake."

Brie took the paper back and crushed it to her chest. "I can't believe he did that! When can we visit Russia again?"

Sir took the deed from her and folded it up carefully, stating, "Not for a quite a while, téa. Somebody has a documentary to introduce to the world."

"Then this must be the first place we visit—after your grandmother's, of course."

"I concur," he said agreeably.

Brie picked up a black envelope with her name neatly printed in silver. She found a photograph inside of a beautiful two-toned flogger of royal purple and black. On the back it read:

> *A gift crafted especially for you. Enjoy its*
> *character, pearl.*
> *Sincerest regards, Marquis*

"I wonder where it is," she mused, realizing that he had been limited by what could be placed on her tray.

"I believe Marquis left a package behind when he left."

"Oh, I can't wait to feel it! Well, maybe I can. I love opening gifts too much," Brie picked up another envelope. She found a wondrous variety of treasures within the cards, from a certificate for a designer leash from Captain to a weekend getaway compliments of Baron.

Mr. Gallant had given her a formal dinner invitation, while Headmaster Coen had arranged a private play session for two at the newest club soon to open in Los Angeles. But Brie's personal favorite was a small framed picture of Sir standing beside Mr. Reynolds and his wife. It had been taken the night of the collaring.

Master Anderson's gift, however, tickled her because it had a humorous element:

> Inside your Master's car—on his seat, in fact—sits an indoor herb garden. This gift will benefit you in two ways, young Brie. Your Master can experience the tranquility of gardening, albeit on a smaller scale, and you can use the fruits of his labors to flavor your ever-improving culinary attempts.
>
> Yours truly, Master Anderson

Brie snickered as she handed over the card for Sir to read.

The last one on the tray was from Mary. Brie was extremely curious as to what Mary would consider an appropriate gift.

> This is my home phone number. I give you permission to call me, night or day. I don't normally give it out, and never to women. Consider yourself privileged, bitch.
>
> ~Mary

Brie giggled, but understood how huge the gift was. Although she already had her cell phone number, giving

Brie access to her home phone was the closest Mary had ever come to treating her like a real friend. She looked at Sir and smiled. "Mary gave me her number."

"Good. I think it's important you two keep in close contact, especially with the documentary coming out. You may need each other's support."

Brie put down the card and stared at him. "Do you really believe my work will be received badly, Sir?"

He played with a lock of her hair. "I believe that you will create polar reactions with it. Some will celebrate you for introducing them to the world of BDSM, while others will revile you for the debauchery you have unleashed on the world. Both reactions will be a challenge, and I want you surrounded by people who will keep you grounded. Miss Wilson is one such person."

Brie realized the gift might not be as personal as she first thought. "Did you suggest that she give me her number, Sir?"

"No, Brie. The only influence I had was in reminding her of your unique journey together. It was her decision to come to the party, as well as the type of gift to bring."

Brie kissed the phone number on the card. "It means a lot that I am the first girlfriend she's ever given her number to. But I must admit I'm tempted to call her at all hours of the night, just to test her resolve."

Sir frowned.

She kissed his downturned lips. "I'm just kidding, Sir. I would never be so immature." She made a mental note not to joke about Mary around him, but she knew Lea would have totally thought that was funny.

Picking up the photo of Sir, Brie stared at his serious,

but gorgeous face. "You look so handsome, Master. I love this picture because it captures that moment before you collared me. You had no idea what was headed your way that night."

He took the photo from her and examined it critically.

Brie traced the outline of his face in the picture. "This is the look of a handsome condor, Sir. One about to claim his mate."

He tickled her ribs, causing her to squeal and squirm. "Such a disobedient little thing she was, too. What the hell was I thinking?"

Condor Devotion

B rie smiled as she listened to the sound of his steady heartbeat. With his arms wrapped around her, she was safe to revel in the afterglow of his lovemaking. These moments were a little taste of heaven on earth.

Sir stirred beneath her. "Let me get up to turn out the lights. Stay here."

Brie's heart started racing when he got up and left the room. This was the opportunity she had been waiting for. She headed directly for the closet and got on her tiptoes to reach for the thin wooden box.

She carried it out and laid it on the bedside table. Taking a deep breath, she undid the latch and opened the lid, then took out the branding iron. In a fluid motion, she turned and knelt facing the door, her head bowed and the iron rod held up in petition.

She bit her lip as she waited for Sir's return, her heart beating like a hummingbird's wings. There was no fear in the offer, simply the deep-seated need to be marked as Sir's.

He entered the room and stopped in his tracks.

"Téa."

She looked up at him from her kneeling position and begged earnestly, "Please…"

He stepped forward and took the brand from her hands. "The pain will be significant, téa. This is not a simple tattoo and cannot be covered up later should you dislike the results."

"I understand, Master."

He knelt down beside her and placed the rod back in her hands. "I cannot guarantee how the brand will heal, or what it will look like afterwards. It may not be pretty."

"Before I made any decisions, I googled it, Sir. I understand the risks." She touched his cheek, which was rough with five o'clock shadow. "I *need* to feel your mark on my skin. I want it to hurt."

"Why?"

She lowered her eyes, unsure if she could clearly explain the desire in her heart. "So that it counts. This brand will mark a profound point in my life…on my body and in my mind. A rite of passage. It will require both strength and courage to receive this brand of yours, but I've never wanted something as much."

Brie felt so strongly that she couldn't bear the thought of him denying her request, so she braved calling Sir by his given name. "Thane, my skin tingles with need of it; my soul cries out for it."

His eyes flashed with an emotion she could not identify. He cleared his throat and said huskily, "You should know I will not be the one to do it. Master Coen is the only one I trust to brand you."

She looked down to hide her smile, pleased her request had been granted.

Sir helped Brie to her feet. "This is as significant as a collaring, téa. I leave it up to you whether you want witnesses."

Brie wrapped her arms around his waist, pressing her cheek against his chest. "Sir, I would like it to be just us, under the stars."

He crushed her against him, but said nothing for several moments. Sir's voice was gruff with emotion when he spoke again. "I will give you a week to reconsider, téa. The passion you feel now may lose its luster as the date approaches."

"With all due respect, Sir, I don't think that will happen."

His fingers lightly caressed the small of her back—the area to be branded. His touch left her lightheaded and tingly all over. Brie sighed in contentment. "I love you, Master."

The night of the branding, Brie felt nothing but peace. There was no question in her mind that this was what she wanted. She'd been curious as to whether the fear of the hot iron would deter her from going through with it, but the reality was that the pain was what attracted her to the act. It wasn't a case of needing the pain for pain's sake; it was the challenge it presented. She wanted to make a great sacrifice to Sir. Even though she was not a masochist, if the act wasn't painful, it would cheapen the gift.

Brie felt akin to a Native American warrior as they drove out to meet Master Coen. She was out to prove her worth by way of a trial she had willingly accepted. It was both thrilling and terrifying.

Sir took her to a secluded beach under the stars where the muscle-bound Headmaster Coen stood waiting for them beside a fire ring with red-hot coals.

Brie briefly glanced at the flames and saw the iron rod nestled in the coals. For the first time she felt a quiver of fear and found it strangely exhilarating.

"Good evening, Davis." He nodded to Brie. "Miss Bennett."

Sir held out his hand. "Thank you for coming tonight."

"I am honored to be part of such a sacred event."

"Yes, thank you, Headmaster Coen," Brie echoed. "It eases my mind, as you and I have been through this once before."

He chuckled lightly. "Unlike last time, Miss Bennett, there will be no mind-fuck. If you get cold feet, you have only to say the word up until the moment the hot iron touches your skin. After that point, I will be committed to giving you a proper brand."

Brie took a nervous breath, the weight of what she was about to do hitting her full force. "I will do everything in my power not to move when that time comes, Master Coen."

"The branding itself is a quick process, but you'll find the challenge comes in the healing afterwards. It will take months for the burns to settle down and up to a year for the brand to heal. You also run the risk of infection. Do you understand what you are committing to?"

"I do, Master Coen. I understand and accept the risks."

"Fine." Master Coen turned to Sir. "I'm satisfied."

"Good." Sir then asked Brie, "Would you like to have a drink in honor of your courage before or after your branding?"

Hearing the word 'branding' spoken so casually caused her loins to contract in fearful pleasure.

I'm really going to do this...

"Afterwards, Sir. I want to be fully aware. I need to embrace this experience, body and soul."

Sir pulled a gag from his pocket. Brie had requested it, feeling it would give her a sense of control to be able to bite down on the cloth and muffle any screams she might make.

Brie turned and opened her mouth, allowing him to tie it securely in place. Afterwards, Sir turned her back to face him, cupping her cheeks in his warm palms. He stared deep into her eyes, caressing her soul with his intense gaze. When he seemed satisfied with her resolve, he commanded, "Undress for me, téa."

Numbness took over as she slowly undressed before the two men. The moment became surreal when she folded her clothes. Master Coen directed her to press her torso against the smooth trunk of a huge tree that had washed ashore. Even lying on its side, the log came up to Brie's waist.

"It will give you the support you need during the

branding," he stated. "If you concentrate on leaning into the trunk, you will avoid flinching and possibly ruining the brand."

Brie pressed her waist against the smooth trunk, surprised that she would not be bound as she had been at the Training Center. Instead, Sir moved around to the other side of the trunk and took hold of both of her hands, his confident smile giving her courage.

She took a moment to glance around her, soaking in the beauty of their surroundings: the small crescent moon, the ghostly white foam of the waves constantly hitting the beach, and the night sky sprinkled with stars. All of it added to this unique moment in time. Brie felt connected to the universe; humans throughout history had performed rituals such as this to mark moments of deep spiritual significance.

"Look into my eyes, téa."

Brie focused her gaze solely on Sir.

He stroked her cheek with one hand while still holding tightly onto her wrists with the other, not breaking their bond. "I brand you tonight not only to mark you as mine, téa, but to celebrate your devotion and courage as my submissive. To others it may symbolize my ownership over you, but to me it announces my undying commitment. There will be no other in my life. Even death will not stand in the way of my commitment to you."

Brie sighed contentedly. She looked into his eyes again, noting the burning flames from the fire reflected in them. *I desire no other man to be Master over me.*

"Are you ready?" Master Coen asked from behind

her.

Brie closed her eyes for a moment. Up until now, it had been a mental surrender. Now it would become a physical one. Still…the peace she felt gave her the courage to nod her head.

The headmaster meticulously cleaned off the area to limit the risk of infection before leaving her side to get the hot iron from the fire.

Sir squeezed her hands tightly and commanded, "Look at me, téa. Do not look away."

Brie opened her eyes, her gag preventing a verbal answer. She hoped to take her brand in brave silence, but was unsure if she would have the strength.

She felt Master Coen approach and held her breath. She stared at Sir, repeating in her head, *This is my outward expression of the love beating inside my heart.*

"It is good you have an expert doing this, Miss Bennett," Headmaster Coen informed her, his voice calm and reassuring. "I know what's needed to provide the desired result without causing excess damage." Coen placed his beefy hand on her small waist and barked, "Do not move."

Brie trembled involuntarily just before he pressed the red-hot metal firmly against the area just above her tailbone. She shrieked into the gag as a white-hot current of pain exploded from her back into her entire body. Despite the extreme pain, Brie kept her eyes open, not wanting to lose contact with Sir—even when the sickening sound of burning skin filled her ears.

Sir's grip kept her grounded and his eyes conveyed pride and courage. It gave her the ability to remain still.

When Master Coen removed the brand, Brie was surprised to feel instant relief. As he carefully put the iron down, the Headmaster informed her, "Your body is in shock. However, it won't take long for the pain to return. Before it does, I'm going to dress the area to keep it free from infection."

He placed a cool cloth on her back and Brie groaned in appreciation, but he soon took it away, explaining as he worked, "I'm placing a special bandage on your skin. It has been soaked in a silver solution to provide an extra layer of protection against infection. As per your Master's request, I will also add compression to the burn. It will help minimize the scarring." While he wrapped a stocking-like garment around her waist, Sir untied her gag.

The lack of pain and the special care being taken had her worried, and she naïvely asked, "I will still have a scar, won't I?"

Master Coen's laughter filled the night air. "You cannot avoid it, Miss Bennett."

Sir gathered her gingerly in his arms, explaining, "Although I want to admire your mark, téa, I would like it to heal as cleanly as possible."

Brie rested her head on his chest, suddenly overtaken by a case of uncontrollable shivering. Shortly after, the pain came back with a vengeance. She began to pant, fighting back the urge to cry at the intensity of it.

Master Coen came to her with ibuprofen and a canteen of water. "It will help with the inflammation, as well as the pain." Brie looked at it warily, unsure whether she should suffer a little longer to prove her devotion.

"Take it, téa," Sir ordered.

That immediately ended any questions she had on the subject. Brie closed her eyes as Sir lifted the canteen and she swallowed the cold water, letting it ease her parched throat.

"It is important you keep hydrated, Miss Bennett," Master Coen instructed. "It will aid the healing process."

Brie bit her lip and nodded, a whimper almost escaping. With each passing minute, she was finding the pain increasingly unbearable.

"Are you ready?" Master Coen asked Sir.

Brie was shocked to see Sir begin unbuttoning his shirt, exposing his handsome chest to the cold night air. "Sir?"

He positioned her to his right as he braced himself against the thickest part of the log.

Brie gasped when she saw Master Coen clean off the area above Sir's heart before picking up a second brand from the fire.

Sir smiled down at Brie. "Why are you surprised? I would never ask you to do something that I was unwilling to do myself."

All the pain she'd been suffering melted away momentarily as she watched Headmaster Coen approach Sir with the new brand. Instead of a capital 'T', it was lowercase to represent Sir's name for her.

"Can I hold your hand, Master?" Brie whispered, suddenly overcome with emotion.

"Yes, téa."

She took his right hand and cradled it in both of hers. He gazed down at Brie with an aura of calm. "I wear this brand as a reminder to you of your place."

"Brace yourself," Master Coen ordered, just before he positioned the brand over Sir's chest muscle and pressed the metal onto the skin above his heart. Sir squeezed Brie's hand hard, but his gaze did not waver and no sound escaped his lips.

The smell of burning hair and skin greeted Brie's nostrils, making her feel woozy. When Master Coen pulled away, Sir let out an energetic grunt and roared, "Fuuuuck!"

He grabbed the back of Brie's neck with his right hand and sought out her lips. He kissed her deeply, stealing the breath from her lungs with his passion.

"Davis, I need to dress the area," Master Coen stated, interrupting their impassioned embrace.

Sir reluctantly pulled away and grinned down at her, his eyes flashing with lustful excitement. "Always the caretaker, isn't he?"

As he cooled the area before placing on the bandage, Master Coen said dryly, "It's what makes me the perfect headmaster. I don't let my emotions get in the way of my duty."

Sir snorted. "Although you may be right in some instances, it does make you a stick-in-the-mud. You might want to loosen up a bit, *Headmaster* Coen."

Master Coen shook his head as he handed Sir the ibuprofen and water. "Says the man who was forced to quit the position because he let his emotions get the better of him."

Sir stated emphatically, "Smartest thing I ever did, Coen."

His lips met Brie's again. She closed her eyes and let herself fly through the swirling emotions of love and agony, proud of the fact she now carried the mark of her Master.

Exchanging Places

The weeks following the branding had a sweetness to them. Even though her brand was excruciatingly painful, each day involved a ritual Brie cherished. She would clean and dress Sir's burn and he, in turn, would care for hers.

It involved lathering the branded area, then carefully removing any discharge before rinsing off and patting the skin dry. Sir did it with such tenderness that it reminded Brie of an aftercare session, and she found that time they spent together pleasurable, which offset the pain.

The day Headmaster Coen gave them both a clean bill of health and declared the first stage of healing complete, Sir surprised Brie with a unique challenge when they returned home.

He placed cuffs, rope, and a Wartenberg wheel on the table next to the Tantra chair and held out the blindfold. "Tonight, we switch roles."

Brie felt butterflies as she took the blindfold from him. "I get to be in control, Sir?"

"Yes, téa."

She looked up at her Master and asked, "Why?"

"As a Dominant, it is crucial to experience submission to understand the psychology behind the dynamic. I believe that for a submissive, it is equally important to understand the role of the Dominant."

She glanced at the blindfold in her hand, her loins stirring at the thought.

Sir continued, "I am curious what you have learned and how you will use that knowledge tonight."

Brie said confidently, "I have had only the best teachers, Sir. I am positive you will enjoy the experience."

He leaned over and stroked her mound as he growled into her ear, "Dominate me."

She groaned, her pussy moistening his fingers with her excitement. Brie pulled away and smiled wickedly as she gave her first instructions. "Remove your shirt and belt, as well as your socks and shoes. Lay them beside the chair neatly and kneel before me."

He kept his eyes on her as he slowly followed her commands. She felt her stomach flutter when he lowered himself to the floor. Brie bit her lip as she put the silk blindfold over his eyes and tied it securely behind his head. She stepped back to admire this new view of her Master. He looked so manly and vulnerable, kneeling down before her with his naked chest and black blindfold.

"Ah, the allure of the unknown. Where will I touch you?" she purred.

A smile played across his lips. It pleased her greatly

that he remembered that he'd used those words on her right after the collaring ceremony.

"I want you to lie on the Tantra chair, Sir, hands above your head."

"On my back or stomach, téa?"

She'd forgotten to be specific in her instructions. "On your back, Sir."

He stood up and felt for the lounger, lying down on it with masculine grace.

Brie bit her lip. *Where to begin?*

She picked up the gold cuffs Rytsar had given her. Would he have ever expected they would be used in this way?

Probably not…

Brie grinned as she moved to the head of the Tantra chair, feeling incredibly wicked as she got ready to bind her Master. Brie's heart raced as she tightened each cuff around one of his wrists. She watched him open and close his fists, getting used to the restriction. It was an unexpected turn-on for her.

Moving back to stand beside him, she carefully straddled the chair so that her pussy hovered just above his cock. "Don't move, Sir…" she commanded before her lips landed on his hairy chest. She left a trail of kisses across his muscled torso, ending with a lick of his right nipple.

But his lips were irresistible, so she kissed her way up to them and claimed them for her own. She started off with light butterfly kisses and then nibbled on his bottom lip. His deep, passionate kisses called to her…but in true Dominant form, she denied her own pleasure to intensify his and pulled away.

"I know what I want," she announced. Brie left the chair and went to the kitchen to get a large strawberry from the pantry. The thought of feeding it to Sir made her quiver inside.

Brie returned and straddled him again, this time pressing herself against his hardening cock. "Open your mouth, Sir."

He did so immediately.

Such a good Master… she thought, warming up to her new role.

Brie put the ripe strawberry to his lips. "Take a bite."

She watched his teeth break the skin of the soft fruit and juice burst forth, covering his lips. She took the strawberry away and leaned over to lick the sweet nectar. "That's very nice, Sir," she complimented, before returning it to his lips. She enjoyed the sensual vision as he took another bite.

But the urge to consume his lips became too much for her. She discarded the rest and kissed him deeply, exploring Sir's mouth, running her tongue over his teeth, and sparring playfully with his tongue. She ground against him as she made love to his mouth.

His hands came down and he encased her in his cuffed embrace, pressing her against his shaft as he moved his pelvis in time with hers.

She tsked. "You are being very bad, Sir." Brie lifted his hands back up above his head and left the lounger to grab the rope. With a loop of the rope and a few quick knots she had picked up from Tono, she had Sir's cuffs secured to the chair so that he could not disobey her again.

"I apologize for my over-enthusiasm, téa."

She was not buying it. "I believe it was willful disobedience. Therefore you must be punished."

She could read amusement in his expression. "As you wish, téa."

Brie picked up the Wartenberg wheel before straddling him again. She ran the spiky wheel over the inside of her own arm to get an idea of what kind of pressure to use. "Ooh…" she gasped, having pressed too hard, leaving tiny but deep indentations on her skin. She would have to use lighter pressure on Sir.

Before she began, she warned, "Feel free to call a safe word at any point, for I will not be asking." It was another one of his best lines.

Sir grinned. "Thank you for the reminder, téa. You have me more than a little curious now."

She answered his curiosity by rolling the sharp wheel over his stomach without warning. He jumped at the wheel's first contact, but forced his muscles to relax even as goosebumps rose on his skin. She felt his erection harden even more underneath her as she continued to mark trails across his stomach with the wicked tool. It was clear that he liked the stimulation of it too much.

"Punishment should not be pleasurable," she observed aloud. She leaned over and put the wheel back on the table, saving it for later.

"I have something more effective in mind." Brie undid his pants and eased Sir's shaft from the confines of his briefs. She pushed the material away so that his handsome cock was exposed.

Using a strategy Tono was famous for, Brie teased Sir's cock. It became her plaything as she stroked it with the lightest of brushes, tickled it with the ends of her hair, and on rare occasion, gave it a chaste kiss on the tip.

Sir's groans and stiff cock let her know that she was having the desired effect.

"Naughty Sirs get teased, not pleased," she warned him.

Brie left the chair again and quietly acquired a piece of ice from the freezer. She didn't want him to have any clue what was coming.

Brie slipped off her panties before climbing onto him again. She wanted Sir to feel her warmth and dragged her wet pussy over the length of his cock, teasing the head of it with her opening before abruptly leaving him.

"Prove yourself worthy, Sir. Do not move," she commanded as she placed the ice on the base of his shaft. His balls immediately responded, retracting from the cold. She watched Sir grit his teeth as he held himself still. Brie slowly dragged the ice up the length of his cock and back down, then she leaned over and licked the cold water that clung to it.

Sir grunted in pleasure, making her stomach flutter again.

Brie retraced his cock with the cube of ice, knowing the thrill that opposite temperatures brought to one's senses. She licked his cock, this time taking the head of his shaft into her warm mouth and sucking hard before letting go.

"You are cruel," he complained lustfully.

Brie grinned, taking it as a compliment. She continued to play with the ice until it had entirely melted. As a parting punishment, Brie took hold of his manhood and slowly descended on it, deep-throating him for only a few seconds before pulling back up.

He groaned again, thrusting his pelvis upwards, silently asking for more.

Brie smiled when she saw the bead of pre-come form on the tip of his cock. It was going to taste delicious.

"Will you be good now, Sir?"

He smiled when he answered, "Yes, téa."

"Lose the smirk when you say that, Sir," she admonished.

She could see him struggle not to smile. It took a few moments before he could say with a straight face, "I will obey, téa."

"Good Master."

Brie wasn't quite ready for their session to be over. "I would like to get another toy, Sir."

Sir corrected her gently, "Reword the statement as a Dominant, téa."

Brie blushed as she rephrased it. "Remain still until I return, Sir."

Knowing that leaving him unattended while bound was unsafe, Brie ran down the hall and quickly gathered the candle and matches. She returned, giggling like a little girl and out of breath.

Brie realized that she wasn't coming off as very dominant. Not wanting to fail her assignment, she set the items down and took a couple of moments to gather herself by closing her eyes. She put herself in Sir's shoes—cuffed and tied down, his eyes blinded and his sex exposed, defenseless… It was her job to heighten the sense of anticipation.

She walked around the lounger slowly, liking the way her heels clicked on the marble floor. "We must remove these clothes," she announced. Brie pulled down his pants and briefs in a rough, swift motion.

Oh, that was sexy, she thought, feeling a sensual rush.

Sir's rock-hard cock affirmed that he felt the same. She denied her need no longer and took a long lick of his cock, savoring the tang of his pre-come. *Soon, Brie, soon…* she assured herself as her pussy pulsated with mounting desire.

She settled down on his cock again, her wet lips encasing him without providing the relief of penetration. She struck a match and lit the candle, letting it burn for several moments to allow the scent of jasmine to fill the air.

Just as she was about to pour it on his chest, Sir remarked, "Téa, you may want to cover the area in massaging oil first, unless your intent is to wax my body hair."

He said it nonchalantly, as if he didn't care one way or the other, but Brie could have died. She could just imagine Sir's body with a crisscross of missing hair after she was finished.

In a calm, Dominant voice, Brie answered, "That was the plan, Sir, but I do not fault you for voicing concern."

She placed the candle on the table and went back into the bedroom closet to procure the needed oil. She came back, taking long, confident strides so that her walk would echo throughout the apartment.

Before returning to his side, she removed all of her clothing, leaving only the stilettos on. Brie rubbed a glistening layer of oil over his chest, stomach, and pelvic area. Then she cleaned off her hands, picked up the burning candle and straddled him again.

Brie leaned down and whispered, "Embrace the hot caress, Sir..." as she slowly poured a small line of wax down his right chest muscle, covering his nipple.

He let out a long breath, but remained still and quiet.

Brie poured a second line, imitating the 't' brand on the left side of his chest. She poured a thicker line down the middle of his torso, starting at his sternum and going all the way down to his lower stomach. When she noticed the hot wax pooling in his belly button, she quickly spread it outward so the heat would not concentrate in that one area and burn him.

Brie shook her head, realizing that being the Dominant was serious business. Even a simple candle could cause harm if she wasn't careful. Although she had said she wouldn't ask, she needed to know. "Color?"

"Green, téa."

She breathed a sigh of relief and poured a second line to cross the giant lowercase 't'.

"I'm marking my territory," she explained.

Brie pushed herself down onto Sir's ankles so she had free access to his entire pelvic region. "I love your cock, Sir."

His passionate groan alerted her that he knew exactly what she meant by that statement. Brie carefully poured a thin line of candle wax down the length of his shaft.

Droplets fell on either side, giving him extra sensation.

She poured the corresponding line of the 't' to mark his groin as hers.

"Now that's sexy," she remarked, blowing out her candle and picking up the Wartenberg wheel.

She rolled the instrument, starting at his knee and slowly trailing it up to his pelvis. This time, Sir moaned loudly. Brie felt a gush of wetness in response to his cry. Instead of asking him to state his color, she observed the thick hardness of his cock.

Just like last time, playing with the Wartenberg wheel seemed to have an erotic effect on him. She trailed it up the opposite thigh, stopping just before she reached his scrotum. His cock twitched of its own accord.

She turned around and lightly rolled it over the sole of his left foot. He gasped, trying hard to keep his foot still. It was entertaining, so she used the instrument on his right sole and received the same response. She used it on various parts of his body, keeping him guessing where stimulation would come next.

Brie was thrilled to see his cock pulsing with each beat of his heart, hard and ready for *her* pleasure. She had denied herself long enough. It was time to fulfill a fantasy she'd held for quite some time…

She rubbed the wax off his cock and cleaned off the oil with a warm cloth. Both actions only added to his sensual torture. Brie kissed his princely shaft, tracing her tongue across the ridge of his cock and tickling his frenulum for added fun.

"Téa…" he groaned.

"Yes, Master. Your time has come," she purred, as

she eased her wet pussy onto his cock and slowly took the fullness of Sir into her body.

He threw his head back. "Oh, God."

"The third day of my training, I had a fantasy about you, Sir."

"You...did?" he panted as she moved up and down on his shaft.

"I did. And now you are going to make that fantasy come true."

He let out a low, tortured groan.

"In my fantasy, I told you not to hold back. To come quickly, thinking only of yourself. I want you to do that now."

He shook his head.

"Yes, Master. I am going to fuck you hard and you are going to come inside me with no hesitation." She added with mirth, "Do you understand?"

He licked his lips before replying with a strained, "I do."

"Good. My greatest pleasure is feeling your hot come inside me, Sir." Brie braced her hands carefully on his chest to avoid the brand. "Give me my pleasure."

Brie began fucking him with abandon, taking him deep and riding him hard.

Sir's back arched and his jaw went slack just before his pelvis began to thrust. Brie cried out as he released his pleasure in savage bursts. She screamed, "Yes! Yes!", forcing him deeper as he delivered his seed.

Chills went through her body, the power of his orgasm overwhelming and erotic. She stopped and laid her head on his chest. Her pussy began pulsing violently as she joined him, her inner muscles contracting around his cock in blessed release.

"That…was…amazing!" she gasped between breaths.

He gave her one final thrust. "I liked your fantasy, téa."

She listened to his rapidly beating heart, trying not to grin like a fool. *What an experience!* Topping Sir had been more exciting than she'd thought, although she was certain she hadn't made a good Domme.

"Undo the cuffs, téa. My hands are losing circulation."

Brie quickly disengaged herself to get the key. She noticed his hands were turning blue, a sign of tight restriction. "I'm sorry, Sir." She rubbed his wrists, trying to aid his circulation.

He chuckled. "No need to worry, little sub. No harm done."

"I never truly understood how hard it is to Dom a scene. It's a lot of responsibility, Sir, even though it has its perks."

He ordered her to straddle him, grabbing her waist and grinding against her. "You did an adequate job for your first time."

"I know I made several mistakes, Sir."

"Knowing your tools and how to use them is essential before you start a scene. But I will say that I was impressed with your use of the Wartenberg wheel."

She rubbed his chest with a pleased smile, gently taking off bits of wax. She admitted, "I thought because I had experienced candles that I knew enough to use them."

"I would have stopped you if I was concerned, baby-girl."

She leaned over and kissed him on the lips. "At least you advised me before I gave you a full body waxing."

"Rookie mistake, and one I was not willing to suffer." Brie's head bounced up and down on his chest with the force of his laughter.

"I'm grateful, Sir. I love your hairy chest."

He pulled the blindfold off. "You have made me ravenous with all your teasing. Now I will require *you* to come, slave." Sir dug his hands into the flesh of her ass and thrust himself deep inside her pussy without warning.

She moaned at the forceful entry but quickly adapted herself to his rhythm.

"I will fuck you hard and fast until that pussy is quivering from overuse."

"Yes, Master. Use me, please…"

Dinner with Gallant

Brie had been working long hours with Mr. Holloway's best film editor, Fehér, as well as his graphics team. The progress they were making was encouraging—so much so that Mr. Holloway had started contacting select theaters, offering them exclusive rights to the initial release. He explained to Brie, "Because it's a documentary, we pick a few key theaters and let word of mouth, as well as carefully placed press releases, draw interest. If I've done my job well, the bigger chains will start asking to show the film in their own theaters once it begins to build steam. Although documentaries are not an easy sell, they're not impossible," he said with a cunning smile. "And I like a good challenge." He exuded the confidence of a Dom, giving Brie pleasant shivers.

The prospect of the upcoming release was exciting, but equally overwhelming. The relentless schedule was starting to wear on Brie. She counted herself lucky when Fehér came down with food poisoning and they all went home early one afternoon. She phoned Sir, who instructed her to take advantage of the break and set up the

Red Phoenix

belated birthday dinner with Mr. Gallant.

She was thrilled to finally be dining with her former teacher and his elegant wife. Brie had never had the chance to get to know the statuesque woman because Mr. Gallant was a private man, mixing his personal life with work as little as possible.

But tonight, as a special gift to her, she would be allowed into their personal lives. It meant the world to Brie. She greatly admired the man who'd been her teacher throughout her six-week training.

Brie undressed except for her beloved collar and waited for Sir at the door, following the ritual greeting he had assigned her at the Training Center. She smiled as she knelt, remembering his command: "Legs closed, arms behind your back so that your breasts are presented for my pleasure."

She bowed her head when she heard him. Sir entered and slowly shut the door behind him. He placed his keys on the counter before putting his hand on her head. Brie felt the familiar jolt of electricity her Master's touch inspired.

His low, commanding voice warmed her spirit. "Stand and serve your Master."

Brie stood up gracefully and looked into his luminous eyes. It was clear he had missed this simple ritual as much as she had due to her long hours working on the film.

"Go to the couch and lean over the arm."

Her heart sped up as she walked to the sofa and pressed her torso against it in an inviting pose for her Master. She purred when she felt his fingers petting her sex.

"I will take my pleasure now," he stated as he unzipped his pants and rubbed his cock up and down her outer lips. Before she was fully ready, he forced himself inside. Brie gasped. The friction and tightness were tantalizing.

He grabbed her hips and thrust with more power. Brie cried out, challenged by his strokes.

It seemed to turn Sir on, and he began fucking her with more gusto.

Brie closed her eyes and threw her head back. This was the exact connection she'd needed, the release her body and soul had longed for over the hectic weeks she'd suffered. Brie wanted to feel the thick release of her Master's come.

She pressed against him and moaned loudly to let him know her pleasure. Sir did not disappoint. Her buttocks rippled with his ardent pounding.

Bliss…

"Good evening, Sir Davis," the diminutive but commanding Dom said when he opened the door.

"Mr. Gallant," Sir replied, shaking his hand firmly.

Mr. Gallant turned to Brie and smiled. "And welcome, Miss Bennett. It's a pleasure to have you join us tonight. The other guests have already arrived and my wife is currently seeing to their needs, otherwise she would have met you at the door as well."

Mr. Gallant led them to a formal dining room. Brie was thrilled to see who was seated at the table. "Captain!"

The older gentleman with the misshapen face and sexy eye-patch stood up. "Miss Bennett, it's good to see you again."

The submissive sitting next to him was even more of a surprise. "Candy, I didn't expect to see you here!" Brie asked Sir, "May I go and hug her, Sir?"

Mr. Gallant corrected Brie. "In my home, we do not adhere to strict formalities. Consider it a vanilla setting and behave accordingly."

Brie was surprised by his request, but honored it. She looked at Sir, who gave her a slight nod.

She scooted around the table to give Candy a big hug. There was no missing the fancy pet collar gracing the girl's neck. Brie grinned. "Seeing you again is like getting an extra birthday present, Candy. I've often wondered what happened to you after you finished training."

Candy's cheeks colored an adorable shade of pink when she looked at Captain. "The night of my graduation ceremony, I was introduced to this gentleman. I have been captivated by him ever since."

Captain patted her chair, giving a silent command for her to sit back down. After Candy and Brie had taken their seats, he explained, "If you remember our night together, Miss Bennett, you may recall how I believed your blonde classmate was better suited for me."

"I remember the night well, sir, but not for that reason."

He chuckled politely. "Kind of you to say, Miss Bennett, but I was rather blunt. It turns out that you were correct. The outer shell of a woman does not matter. It is the heart that defines her." He looked at Candy thoughtfully. "I have never encountered such a loyal or tender-hearted creature." He petted her hair lightly. "She just happens to be a comely little thing as well."

Candy closed her eyes and leaned into his caress. It was easy to see she was equally enamored with him.

"To be honest, Candy," Brie explained, "when I saw you scening with Tono at The Haven a while back, I wondered if the two of you were a couple. I never suspected the Captain would be the one to capture your heart." She suddenly realized that sounded rude and added, "But he is a most wonderful choice."

Candy's eyes sparkled when she told Brie, "Captain wanted me to be certain, and allowed me the pleasure of many Doms before he consented to collar me as his pet."

"Youth should not be wasted on one as old as me," Captain stated.

Candy shook her head, smiling at him. It was a tender way to disagree with his statement. "Fortunately, Captain eventually came to the same conclusion I did." She touched his deformed face and said with confidence, "I was born to be his pet."

"Did I miss the formal collaring ceremony?" Brie asked, concerned her hectic life had prevented her from being at such a momentous event.

Captain answered for Candy. "No, Miss Bennett. I have no need for such pomp and circumstance. A commitment between us in private is as binding as any communal ceremony."

"I quite agree," Sir interjected.

Brie looked at Candy again, marveling at her youthful, glowing appearance. "You know, you don't even look like the same girl I met on the light rail."

"I'm *not*. My whole life has changed since my training." She glanced at Captain again. "I never dreamed a Dom could love or care for me so well."

Captain lifted her chin up, gazing into her eyes. He stated proudly, "I enjoy spoiling my pet." It was sweet to see their blossoming connection.

Mr. Gallant guided his wife over to Brie and said, "Miss Bennett, I feel remiss. I have not introduced you formally to my beautiful wife."

Brie faced the exotic Amazon, whose dark brown skin contrasted beautifully against Mr. Gallant's pale skin. Their difference in height contrasted with equal and complementing severity.

"Miss Bennett, this is Ena. My wife and companion of fifteen years."

The submissives bowed to each other. Brie almost felt she was in the presence of royalty because of how elegantly Ena held herself, and how respectfully Mr. Gallant treated her.

Ena's voice was warm and dignified. "It is an honor to have you grace our home tonight, Miss Bennett. My husband has spoken fondly of you on numerous occasions."

"Truly, the honor is mine," Brie replied. "Your strong marriage is an inspiration to me."

Brie noticed Sir looked at her strangely. Had she spoken out of turn?

Ena's smile was enchanting. "That is kind of you to say, but it is my husband I must thank. He cares for me well."

"Nonsense, Ena," Mr. Gallant corrected. "Your intelligence and grace cover any inadequacies I bring to the table."

The beauty blushed and looked at Mr. Gallant coyly.

"And she remains modest to this day. Is it any wonder I cherish her?" He took his wife's hand and kissed it.

Her eyes held a look of such intense love that it touched Brie deeply. To still have that much respect and passion for one another after fifteen years together... She sat down beside Sir, feeling warm from their happiness.

"Should I get the girls now, Husband?" Ena asked Mr. Gallant.

Brie blurted out, "You have children?"

Ena smiled. "Yes, two young girls, aged eight and twelve."

Brie returned the smile, surprised and pleased by the revelation.

"Miss Bennett, it is the reason we keep to an informal protocol in our home. What looks informal to the outsider is actually formal between the two of us. We have transformed everyday phrases, titles and actions to have personal significance to us."

"That's ingenious," Brie complimented. "You can go anywhere and still remain as formal as you desire, even in public."

Mr. Gallant nodded. "It was born out of necessity. Raising two girls, it was important to us to keep our D/s life separate from them."

"But why?" Brie asked, intrigued.

"We both believe that someone who chooses this lifestyle should do it because it is an inner calling, not simply because they were exposed to it as children. I will be fine if my girls grow up and do not venture into this lifestyle. As long as they find mates who treat them with respect and love, I will be satisfied."

Sir inquired, "And if they decide to seek D/s?"

Ena replied with a pleased smile, "Then they couldn't have a better teacher than their father, could they?"

Brie was curious. "Is it difficult living this lifestyle with a young family, Mr. Gallant?"

"It takes careful planning and constant communication. Just like any marriage, children are a huge commitment. At times, their needs must supersede your own. However, that cannot be allowed to consume the marriage itself. For a D/s relationship—for any relationship, really—the partners must cut out time to care for and support one another. It's essential."

Captain put his arm around his pet. "Luckily, that is not something the two of us must worry about."

"Yes, Captain. We have many years to play," Candy agreed, fingering her new collar.

Brie lightly touched her own, and smiled to herself. She remembered when it used to rub against her neck, reminding her of its presence. Over the months, it had become a part of her. The only time she noticed it now was when Sir took it off for certain scenes. Those times that he did made her realize how safe she felt when the collar was securely around her neck, and how vulnerable she felt without it.

"So should I get them, Husband?" Ena politely asked again, with a slight bow of her head.

"Please do, my wife. I am certain they will enjoy meeting our guests."

When the two young ladies entered the dining room, they instantly ran to Mr. Gallant. "Daddy!"

The honest affection was endearing. Brie noted that the girls had an exotic beauty common with the mixing of races. Incredibly, the two girls were even more striking than their mother.

After formal introductions, the girls sat down on either side of Mr. Gallant. As Ena was placing the first of the dishes on the table, Candy suddenly said, "Oh, wait!"

Everyone stared at her.

"Um… You see, I have something for Miss Bennett." She quickly slid a business card over to Brie.

Brie picked it up with trembling fingers. It was worn at the edges, but still intact.

Candy apologized, "It isn't in the same shape as when you gave it to me. You see, I held it many times those weeks before training."

Brie looked down and smiled when she read:

The Submissive Training Center
25 Years of Excellence

Sir looked at its ragged condition and offered, "I have several in my wallet if you would like a new one,

Brie."

Brie held it to her heart and closed her eyes in contented bliss. The card had made it back home...

"I meant to give it to you sooner," Candy explained, "but I kept forgetting. I knew how special it was to me and assumed by the wear when I got it that you might want it back."

Brie opened her eyes, suddenly feeling a little foolish. "No problem. It was yours to keep, but I'll admit I'm thrilled to have it in my hands again."

Sir chuckled. "All this sentimentality over a business card?"

"This is the one you gave me, Sir."

"Is it now?" he said, taking it from her. "Well, if that's the case, maybe we should frame it."

She had been thinking the same thing. "That would be lovely, Sir."

He laughed, kissing the top of her head. "I was only joking, but if it means that much to you, I'll frame it myself." He tucked the card in his wallet, which he then placed back in his suit jacket. When he glanced back at her, he gave a private wink.

Her heart did a flip-flop. Could she love the man more?

Best Intentions

It had been a month since her birthday party, but what had happened between Ms. Clark and Rytsar still bothered Brie. Sir had always maintained that no questions were off limits, so one morning while she was straightening the kitchen, she inquired casually, "Sir, may I ask what happened between Rytsar and Ms. Clark? It was shocking to see her bow in front of him."

Sir gave an irritated sigh. "Durov knew you would eventually ask. He's given me permission to speak about it, because he was upset that your special night had been tainted by her unseemly display."

"But it wasn't his fault, Sir. I don't blame Rytsar. If you feel it's best I remain in the dark, I trust your judgment and will not ask again."

"It was for his sake that I have kept silent. I can only give you minimal details, but not one word can be repeated."

"I give my word not to tell anyone, Sir."

His eyes narrowed with anger when he started speaking. "I'm furious that she put him in that position in front of so many. It was inappropriate and manipulative. All these years I have supported her, but she pulled that even after I warned her not to."

"It seems she still has deep feelings for Rytsar."

"You may be surprised to know it was mutual in the beginning. The sexual attraction between the two was tangible. I remember how surprised I was, as they are both uncompromising personalities, but Dominants have been known to partner up. It's not unheard of, simply unusual."

Brie was more than a little startled to hear that Rytsar had once been attracted to the stern Dominatrix. "Hard to imagine either of them being willing to submit to the other."

He nodded. "Rytsar was an uncompromising Dominant even then, having been raised since adolescence to indulge in his sadistic ways."

"What do you know of Ms. Clark's background, Sir?"

Sir was curt with his reply. "It's irrelevant to the conversation, Brie. Suffice to say she took pride in her skills as a Dominatrix. Durov had failed to pursue her in the manner she was accustomed to and she felt slighted. It was her misplaced pride that caused what happened that night."

Brie was almost afraid to find out—afraid that knowing might break her heart.

Uninterrupted, Sir continued, "I wasn't there when it happened, so I can only speak to what I witnessed. I knew Durov had gone off to celebrate the end of semester finals, so I was unconcerned I hadn't seen him the entire night.

"But around two in the morning I passed by his dorm room and heard muffled screaming. It was low and masculine—men were not something Durov was known to indulge in. When no one answered the door, I was forced to break the lock. I found him bound to his bed, gagged and tortured. His angry screams indicated it had not been consensual."

Sir looked away. "What had happened had scarred him as a man. It came as a shock when I discovered who'd done it."

When he turned back to Brie, his mouth was a hard line. She could tell it was difficult for Sir to speak about it, but he continued anyway. "After taking care of his physical wounds, I went seeking justice."

"I found Samantha crying in a corner of her room. Two things quickly became evident: she was drunk, and she was horrified by what she had done.

"In no way did it excuse her abuse, but she explained how she'd found Durov passed out outside his dorm when she was stumbling home after her own overindulgence. She'd helped him to his bed, where he'd passed out again. Seeing him helpless like that had done something to her. She'd suddenly got a wild hair up her ass to prove she was Domme enough to take him, convincing herself that if he experienced one session with her she'd win over his affections once and for all.

"After tying him up and gagging him so he couldn't resist, she'd woken him. According to her, Durov had remained unyielding the entire time, unwilling to give in to her dominance. In her drunken state, she'd become fixated on breaking his resolve. They'd fought a battle of wills where neither had come out the victor. She had left, furious she hadn't been able to break his ironclad will. What she'd failed to realize was that she had broken him in the worst way possible."

Brie stopped her work in the kitchen and sat down, horrified, imagining a myriad of reprehensible scenarios.

"Although he had every reason to press charges, he refused. He fell into a deep depression and almost quit college. Thankfully, that fierce Russian spirit kicked in and he eventually crawled out of his darkness and continued on with his schooling."

"What happened to Ms. Clark?" Brie asked, hoping for some kind of retribution.

"Samantha begged Durov to forgive her. She spent extensive time in counseling, gave up drinking and, per my suggestion, submitted to a well-known Domme for several months to experience submission for herself. She wanted to prove that she was repentant. Although it came as no consolation to my friend, it molded Samantha into an exceptional Domme."

"I take it he never did forgive her."

"None of her actions fazed Durov. As far as he was concerned, she was dead to him. He continued on as if it had never happened. When the two met in public settings, he simply ignored her. We all assumed he had moved on, but one night he flipped out for no apparent reason and pushed Samantha to the ground. He wrapped his hands around her neck and tried to squeeze the life out of her. I was barely able to break the stranglehold he had." Sir closed his eyes. "I came close to losing them both that night."

The pain Sir still carried was apparent to Brie, but she couldn't understand why he felt responsible.

Sir finished his account by stating, "Durov went back to Russia the next day. He claimed that time and distance were the only things that would prevent him from killing her."

Brie looked at Sir and dared to ask, "I don't understand, Sir. Why did you remain friends with Ms. Clark after she hurt Rytsar so seriously?"

He gave a long sigh of deep regret. "I was her mentor, Brie. I introduced Samantha to BDSM."

It would be difficult to keep such a shocking revelation to herself when she met with Lea and Mary the next day, but Brie refused to betray Sir's or Rytsar's trust. Instead, she planned to concentrate on discovering what was going on between Lea and Tono. She also wanted to find out what had happened to the note Sir's mother had tried to deliver through Faelan during Brie's birthday party. Mary should be able to satisfy her curiosity on that count.

Brie decided to meet the girls at the bar they had frequented when they had been training. It brought back a flood of enjoyable memories.

John, the head bartender, sidled up to them, looking Mary over with a flirtatious grin. "Long time no see, gorgeous." He turned to Brie and asked, "What happened to the long trenchcoats, Brie? I kind of miss the

Goth look on you fine ladies."

Mary, who loved to torment members of the opposite sex, out-and-out lied. "I insisted we come here today. I missed…" she gave him a breathtaking come-hither look, "…the place."

"Well, I'm honored. Just for that, your drink's on the house."

Brie rolled her eyes. Mary was a ruthless user and abuser of her looks, but for some reason men just ate it up.

Once the drinks had been delivered, Brie asked, "So Lea, out with it. What the heck is going on with Tono?"

"Before I spill the beans, I have a joke for you."

Mary groaned. "No, not another one of your lame-ass jokes."

Lea smiled eagerly at Brie. "You know you're kinky when you keep Christmas lights up in your house to hide the real reason you have all those hooks in your home."

"That wasn't bad," Brie said, giggling as she noticed the small white lights over the bar. She poked Lea in the ribs as she asked, "Hey, John, why do you still have Christmas lights up?"

He gave her a goofy grin. "Eh, too lazy to take them down."

"I bet," Lea replied with an exaggerated wink.

"I don't know these two," Mary exclaimed as she moved to a seat farther away.

Lea turned her back on Mary in silent protest and smiled mischievously at Brie as she took a sip of her drink. "So Brie, you're the one who set Tono and me up. Why are you surprised we're together now?"

Mary scooted back over, shaking her head. "Something's not right here. You can't go from lusting over Ms. Clark to cozying up with Jute Freak."

Lea gave her a superior look. "I'll have you know we're living together, Miss Smarty Bitch."

Brie choked on her merlot and started coughing. "Wait. What?"

Lea just grinned and took another drink. It was obvious she was enjoying herself and had no plans to hurry her explanation.

Mary set her rum and Coke down. "Let me get this straight. Not only are you working with Tono, doing Kinbaku demonstrations, but you have partnered up and are living with him?"

"Why is that so shocking?" Lea asked, sounding offended.

Brie's coughing had ceased and she was finally able to speak. "This is the same girl who wants to explore everything while she's young and unattached? Seriously, Lea, how can you go from *that* to settling down with one Dom?"

Mary laughed unkindly. "I think I hear a little jealousy. You know you can't keep them all, Brie."

"It's not jealousy you hear, Mary. It's utter disbelief." Brie turned back to Lea. "What's the real story, girlfriend?"

Lea pouted. "You guys are no fun. I should have been able to run with this for weeks." When neither girl responded, she sighed. "Fine. Tono thought our sessions would go smoother and be more indicative of a genuine Kinbaku partnering if we got to know each other. He insists that Kinbaku is best showcased when the couple is in sync."

Brie lifted her glass. "I'd drink to that."

"So…kind of going along the lines of what you did with Tono, I suggested a temporary contract. I've been kind of curious what full-time subbing is like." She shrugged and smiled. "Besides, who wouldn't want to be trained by the sexy jute Master?"

"Me!" Mary stated emphatically. "I hate that weird rope crap."

"I take it Tono was agreeable?" Brie asked, still adjusting to the fact Lea and Tono were living together.

"He was hesitant at first. But after a couple of days he came up with a contract for me to sign."

"How long is it for?" Brie pressed, wondering if Lea was pulling her leg.

"Until the end of our classes together."

Mary snickered. "Just look at Brie trying to act all calm, but inside she's boiling over with jealousy. Admit it!"

Brie said coolly, "I'll admit no such thing. I'm surprised, yes, but jealous? No. I want Tono to be happy." She slid her hand over and squeezed her best friend's. "And, of course, I want Lea happy as well. It's just that I don't see you two as a match. I would hate either of you to get hurt by this temporary partnering."

Lea giggled. "Not everyone falls in love with the Doms they work with, Brie. You're just a hopeless romantic. I see it more as a business transaction. He gets a devoted sub—who can cook, by the way—and I get to be trained by a true master of the art. It's quite exciting, actually. This twenty-four seven stuff is really demanding, though. It's like you said, Brie—I'm learning new things about myself on a daily basis."

Brie nodded. "Isn't that the truth…?"

Lea clicked her tongue at Mary. "You should give it a try. Might mellow you out some."

Blonde Nemesis snarled. "Me, tied down? Not going to happen even for a month. This is the time to fly free, girls. To experience the world while you can. No one controls me unless I want them to. I wouldn't have it any other way. You're both idiots, but Brie's the worst."

Brie huffed. "Just because you can't commit doesn't make commitment wrong. Stop belittling my choice."

Mary's nostrils flared as she built up to an ugly outburst. John stopped by to check on them and noticed. "Looks like you could use another drink there, gorgeous."

Mary flashed him a fiery glare.

"Yep," he said nonchalantly, unfazed by her venomous stare. He hit the counter twice with his fist. "Looks like you could use a double."

As he walked away, Brie called, "You're the best, John."

Mary's ugly stare landed on her. It seemed like the perfect time to ask, "So Mary Quite Contrary, whatever happened to that note?"

Surprisingly, Mary's countenance completely changed and she smiled. "Faelan and I decided to have a little fun and froze it in a block of ice. We sent it back to that Elizabeth woman with a message. 'Will deliver when hell freezes over.'"

Lea laughed. "Funny, but harmless. Good one, Mary."

"Know what the cow did?"

Brie suddenly got a sick feeling in the pit of her stomach. "What?"

"She sent it back nestled in an ice chest, still encased in the cube of ice."

Brie frowned, sensing there was more. "Was that all?"

"No. She included her own little note. 'Hell may come sooner than you think.'"

"Whoa…" Lea exclaimed. "That's an ominous threat if I ever heard one."

Brie's heart started racing as the hairs rose on the back of her neck. She imagined Ruth's cruel but beautiful face, and felt a protective surge shoot through her veins. She would do *anything* to protect her friends.

"Mary, I'm sorry she involved you and Faelan in her scheming. It's not right, but nothing about that woman is right." Despite her anger, Brie also felt a pang of sympathy for Sir's mother. What if the crazy woman was truly dying and felt she had to resort to threats out of sheer desperation?

"I would like the letter. If it is in my hands, she won't have any reason to threaten you again."

"I'm big enough to care for myself, Brie," Mary answered irritably.

"I won't be able to rest until I've destroyed the damn thing myself. Please, Mary. Do this for me."

Mary shrugged. "You're a fool, Brie, but I'll let you nail your own coffin shut if you insist."

Lea growled, "Why are you always so negative, Mary?"

"Why are you such a ditz, Lea?"

Brie could sense that they were all on edge. There was no point in prolonging their suffering. Besides, the sooner she got rid of the offending note, the better.

"Do you mind if we go now?"

"And end this lovely girl-chat?" Mary snarked.

Lea stood up. "A minute less of you would be a gift." She gave Brie a big hug. "If you need me for any reason, call. You hear me?"

Brie laid her head against Lea's large bosom for a moment, liking the feeling of being nurtured that flooded over her. "I will, girlfriend."

"Come on, Brie-a-licious. Let's get this over with."

The two drove to Mary's apartment, where Mary retrieved the icebox. She opened it and whistled. "Must be a high quality cooler—the ice has hardly melted."

Brie took it and set it on the passenger seat of her car, slamming the door shut. "The sooner it's gone, the better for everyone."

Just before she drove off, Mary stopped her. "I think you're making a mistake getting involved in this."

Brie shook her head. "You don't understand, Mary. I would do anything for Sir. *Anything.*"

"I know Bouncy Boobs already said this, but I'll say it anyway. If you need me, call."

Brie waved off Mary's concern and jumped in the car. As she made her way back home, she kept glancing at the cooler. It reminded her a little of Pandora's box. Inside were words Sir's mother wanted him to see. Were they words full of hate or healing?

She knew Sir was off meeting with clients for the day, which was part of the reason she'd asked to see her friends. Thankfully, that left her plenty of time to get rid of the note. She hurried up the stairs and turned on the faucet full blast as soon as she entered the kitchen. Brie slid the heavy block of ice under the heated water and waited, pacing around the kitchen. She became nervous when it seemed to be taking too long. Even though Sir wasn't due back for hours she wanted the note, and any evidence of it, long gone by the time he came home.

Brie, why did you bring it here? she chided herself as she watched the ice block slowly melt. But she knew why…

She needed to know if the note held hope. Was it possible for Sir to make some semblance of peace with his mother before she died? It was Brie's greatest wish to help make that happen if she could. *No one is completely evil,* she thought. *Every person has goodness in them.* She was convinced that the threat of death could bring clarity to the darkest of hearts.

After what felt like forever, Brie got out a kitchen towel and laid what remained of the cube on the table. She searched through the pantry until she found the toolbox Sir kept there. She grabbed the hammer and started hacking at the ice.

At first it seemed unbreakable, but once the cracks started the ice fell away in shards. As Brie got closer to the center, she noticed that Mary hadn't covered the letter in any protective material. More likely than not, the letter inside would be unreadable.

Maybe it's for the best…

But Brie's curiosity was too great. She continued to hack away until the envelope was free. She stared at it for several seconds before grabbing the scissors and carefully cutting off the top. She felt like a criminal, but there was no stopping now. She *had* to know.

Holding her breath, Brie drew out the folded note and opened it. It was smeared, but still legible.

Thane,

If my impending death means nothing to you, perhaps your father's violin will. If you do not consent to meet, I will destroy the violin. Yes, that damn instrument that has been in the family for centuries. It will cease to exist, just like your father.

So you see, son, Mommy has you by the balls.

Time to play by my rules.

"What are you doing?"

Brie jumped, her heart threatening to burst at being caught. She put the letter down by her side and turned to face Sir. "I thought you were out…"

"I had a severe headache and decided to come home today to sleep it off. Little did I suspect my own sub would bang a worse headache into my brain. Now answer the question."

"I… I—" The tears started to fall.

"Is that from her?" he stated in a deceptively calm voice.

She nodded, her throat closed too tightly to allow speech.

"I won't even ask how it ended up in such a state." Sir's eyes bored into her with a coldness that stabbed her very soul. "You have betrayed me on a level I'd never thought possible." Sir strode over and took the note from her, crumpling it into a wad before turning on the gas stove.

Brie managed to blurt out, "She'll destroy the violin!"

He hesitated for a second before throwing the paper onto the flame. It took a while to catch fire, but soon the whole kitchen was filled with the faint smell of the burning paper.

He growled darkly under his breath after the note had burned itself out, and then turned on Brie. His gaze was clouded with anger. "I commanded you not to have any contact with her and yet I find you here, seeking out her correspondence behind my back. I have purposely disregarded every attempt at contact and then you do this…"

Brie was desperate to explain. "Sir, I wanted to destroy the note myself."

"The fact you disobeyed my orders on something so vital speaks volumes, Miss Bennett."

Brie whimpered, knowing the use of her surname was a bad omen. "Sir, she threatened Mary and Faelan for not delivering her message. I wanted to protect them and you from its contents. But before I destroyed it, I was overcome with hope that she wanted to make things right by you."

"Things will *never* be right between us!" he shouted.

Brie fell to the floor, bowing in supplication. "I'm sorry, Sir."

He asked, his voice as cold as ice, "Do you realize what you have done?"

She shook her head with her forehead still pressed to the floor.

"You have forced me to react. Had you simply destroyed it, I would be ignorant of her plan and unable to stop it. I thought she had gotten rid of the instrument years ago. Now I am obligated to liberate my father's violin from the beast."

She said in the barest of whispers, "You could pretend you don't know."

"No, Miss Bennett. That is something I *cannot* do." She heard him pull out his phone and speak into it. "Yes, it's me. Simply state where and when. No, I will not." He paused for a moment, then snarled, "If it is a requirement then I must acquiesce." He ended the call, and threw the phone onto the table.

"Get off the floor and clean up the mess you've made."

The apartment was full of a black rage that hung in every corner; there was no escaping it, even when Sir retired to the bedroom.

After Brie had finished restoring the kitchen to order, she took the ice chest and went to the basement garage to throw it in the dumpster. It didn't ease her misgivings, but she couldn't bear to have anything of that woman's near her.

She clearly understood Sir's intense rage, now that she had read his mother's hateful words, but it gutted her to know his anger was also directed towards her now.

As the rays of the sun disappeared behind the horizon, Sir emerged from their room. His haggard expression alerted her to the fact he was still suffering from a debilitating headache.

"Miss Bennett, I think it best that you find a place to stay tonight. Call me at noon so I can pick you up. You presence has been requested at the meeting tomorrow."

"Sir, I never meant—"

He turned from her to return to the bedroom. "I will need to meditate if I am to survive tomorrow. Goodnight." She heard him quietly shut the door.

With a trembling hand, she dialed and then sobbed into the phone, "Mary... I fucked up bad..."

Can their love survive what lies ahead?

Find out in the next part of Brie's journey, *Hold Me*.

Buy the next in the series:

#1 (Teach Me)

#2 (Love Me)

#3 (Catch Me)

#4 (Try Me)

#5 (Protect Me)

#6 (Hold Me)

#7 (Surprise Me)

Brie's Submission series:

You can find Red on:
Twitter: @redphoenix69
Website: RedPhoenix69.com

 Keep up to date with the newest release of Brie by signing up for Red Phoenix's newsletter: redphoenix69.com/newsletter-signup

Red Phoenix is the author of:

Blissfully Undone
* Available in eBook and paperback
(Snowy Fun—Two people find themselves snowbound in a cabin where hidden love can flourish, taking one couple on a sensual journey into ménage à trois)

His Scottish Pet: Dom of the Ages
* Available in eBook and paperback
Audio Book: *His Scottish Pet: Dom of the Ages*
(Scottish Dom—A sexy Dom escapes to Scotland in the late 1400s. He encounters a waif who has the potential to free him from his tragic curse)

The Erotic Love Story of Amy and Troy
* Available in eBook and paperback
(Sexual Adventures—True love reigns, but fate continually throws Troy and Amy into the arms of others)

eBooks

Varick: The Reckoning

(Savory Vampire—A dark, sexy vampire story. The hero navigates the dangerous world he has been thrust into with lusty passion and a pure heart)

Keeper of the Wolf Clan (Keeper of Wolves, #1)

(Sexual Secrets—A virginal werewolf must act as the clan's mysterious Keeper)

The Keeper Finds Her Mate (Keeper of Wolves, #2)

(Second Chances—A young she-wolf must choose between old ties or new beginnings)

The Keeper Unites the Alphas (Keeper of Wolves, #3)

(Serious Consequences—The young she-wolf is captured by the rival clan)

Boxed Set: Keeper of Wolves Series (Books 1-3)

(Surprising Secrets—A secret so shocking it will rock Layla's world. The young she-wolf is put in a position of being able to save her werewolf clan or becoming the reason for its destruction)

Socrates Inspires Cherry to Blossom

(Satisfying Surrender—a mature and curvaceous woman
becomes fascinated by an online Dom who has much to
teach her)

By the Light of the Scottish Moon

(Saving Love—Two lost souls, the Moon, a werewolf
and a death wish…)

In 9 Days

(Sweet Romance—A young girl falls in love with the new
student, nicknamed 'the Freak')

9 Days and Counting

(Sacrificial Love—The sequel to In 9 Days delves into
the emotional reunion of two longtime lovers)

And Then He Saved Me

(Saving Tenderness—When a young girl tries to kill
herself, a man of great character intervenes with a love
that heals)

Play With Me at Noon

(Seeking Fulfillment—A desperate wife lives out her
fantasies by taking five different men in five days)

Connect with Red on Substance B

Substance B is a platform for independent authors to directly connect with their readers. Please visit Red's Substance B page where you can:

- Sign up for Red's newsletter
- Send a message to Red
- See all platforms where Red's books are sold

Visit Substance B today to learn more about your favorite independent authors.

CPSIA information can be obtained
at www.ICGtesting.com
Printed in the USA
LVOW04s1958211016

509751LV00008B/421/P